Love at the Icicle Café

Love at the Icicle Café

Denise N. Wheatley

Love at the Icicle Café

Tule Publishing First Printing, December 2020

The Tule Publishing, Inc.

First Publication by Tule Publishing 2020

Cover design by LLewellen Designs

ISBN: 978-1-952560-77-4

Dear Reader,

Happy holidays to you and yours! Thank you so much for joining me on Mina and Scott's journey in LOVE AT THE ICICLE CAFÉ. Developing these characters and telling their stories was such a pleasure, as was watching them transform from the first page to the last.

LOVE AT THE ICICLE CAFÉ takes place in the snowy, fictitious town of Gosberg, Germany. I was inspired to create this cozy community by my father, who was based in Germany while serving in the U.S. military.

Another fun fact: Mina is a patent attorney who loves to bake, and Scott is a gourmet chef. By the time I'd finished writing this book, I had deemed myself an expert in both patent law *and* German cooking! ☺

I hope you enjoy reading LOVE AT THE ICICLE CAFÉ as much as I loved writing it. If you'd like to learn more about me and stay up-to-date on my new releases, here's where you can find me: On Instagram: @denise_wheatley_writer, on Twitter: @DeniseWheatley. My author blog is www.denisenwheatley.com. I love chatting with readers and look forward to connecting with you!

Thank you for your support, and happy reading!
Denise N. Wheatley

P.S. Keep an eye out for my contemporary romance series, A FEARLESS FAIRYTALE, coming in early 2021!

Chapter One

"I'M SO GLAD I was able to help you win your case," patent attorney Mina Richards said.

"We wouldn't have been able to do it without you," Jim Stern, owner of Colorblind Solution Lenses, replied. "Trust me, the next time we need to hit someone with an infringement claim, I'll be giving you a call."

Mina led Jim through the lobby of Anderson & Moore LLP. "Thank you. It would be my pleasure to represent you again," she said, shaking his hand before he exited the law firm.

She spun on her heel and practically floated toward her office. On the way there, she was stopped by Stephen Anderson, who'd cofounded the firm along with his partner, Mitchell Moore.

"Good job, Miss Richards. That was a huge victory you just pulled off."

She smiled proudly while pulling her sleek chestnut brown locks behind her ear. "Thank you, sir. I worked really hard on this one."

"And it showed. Keep it up. You never know what good

things may be awaiting you here at the firm."

Mina's smile widened as she watched Stephen walk away through gleaming eyes.

"Like making partner," she murmured to herself just as Karen, her best friend and legal assistant, rushed over and grabbed her arm.

"Congratulations, girl! You are *amazing*."

"Aww, thanks sis. Come on. Let's go celebrate. I've got goodies."

Karen rubbed her hands together as they strolled to her office. "Ooh, my mouth is already watering."

"Have a seat," Mina said. She reached inside her drawer and pulled out a two-tier container filled with a variety of colorful gourmet cupcakes.

"Wow," Karen breathed. "These are gorgeous." She grabbed a chocolate treat topped with French buttercream frosting. "Don't tell my trainer."

"Tell him what?" Mina asked, giving her a wink.

"See, that's why I love you." Karen took a big bite out of the cupcake and closed her eyes. "*Mm.* This is delicious. Nothing in life should be this good. How is it that you're such an excellent attorney *and* baker? Where did you learn such sorcery?"

Mina giggled while picking up a red velvet cupcake and swiping a dollop of icing off the top. "I get it from my mama. You know she's a wizard in the kitchen. I held on to everything she taught me at her café when we lived in

Germany."

"Well, she was a master teacher."

"That she was..." Mina gazed down at the cupcakes. "We had some great times back at The Icicle Café."

"I think it's so cool that your parents opened a winter-themed restaurant overseas while your father served in the army."

"Yeah, it's a pretty amazing place. That café has always been such a beloved staple within the Gosberg community.

"Do you ever miss being in Gosberg, even though it's the complete opposite of sunny Clover, California?"

Mina bit into her cupcake and glanced out the window at the swaying palm trees. "You know, I do miss it sometimes. The beautiful snowfalls, the townspeople that felt like family...there's a small-town coziness to Gosberg that you just don't get living in the city."

"That sounds so nice. Do your parents still own the café?"

"They do, along with the Dawson family. After my father retired from the army, we moved to Clover and the Dawsons stayed in Gosberg to manage it. These days their son Scott does most of the managing. But there've been rumblings that the café might be sold because the Dawsons want to move back to the states."

Mina was interrupted when her cell phone buzzed. When the name Calvin Michaels popped up on the screen, a dimpled grin spread across her face.

"I know what that look means," Karen mumbled through a mouthful of frosting. "A text from Mr. Michaels must be coming through."

"As a matter of fact, it is." Mina typed in her security code and tapped the message.

Hey love. Hope you're having a wonderful day. I'm already guessing you won your case. Can't wait to see you tonight at dinner. I've got BIG news…

Mina took another bite of her cupcake then wrote Calvin back.

Hey honey. I actually did win big in court today. Can't wait to hear your news. Based on the convo I just had with Stephen, I may be getting some great news soon, too. See you tonight. XO

Mina looked up at Karen, who was reaching inside the container for another cupcake. "If you do that, I'm gonna have to tell your trainer."

Karen squinted her eyes then turned her nose up at Mina's svelte, Pilates-honed figure. "*Fine*," she grunted. "I'll pass. They're just so hard to resist. You shouldn't be such a good baker! Anyway, what's up with Calvin?"

"We're getting together for dinner tonight. Apparently, he's got something pretty exciting to share with me. I think he's been named partner at the law firm where he works."

"Really? That's awesome!" Karen stared across the desk at Mina, her eyes shining with admiration. "You're really living the dream, you know that? I mean, you're an incredible attorney who's dating an incredible attorney, you're both going to be partners at your firms, and I'm convinced that

Calvin is going to propose any day now. You two are about to take over the world."

"Thanks, Kay. And that sounds really good. But in all honesty, patent law is starting to feel so...*mundane* to me. I've been craving a little more excitement and creativity in my career. I'm hoping that once I make partner, I'll have more control over my caseload and can choose cases that'll hold my interest."

"Wait, you're looking for excitement and creativity in patent law? Good luck with that."

"I'm just trying to be positive since I've put so much time and energy into my career. Oh, and by the way, when I was talking with Stephen just now, he complimented me on my Colorblind Solutions win and said there are *good things* waiting for me here at the firm."

"Yes!" Karen squealed, holding her hand in the air and giving Mina a high five. "Word around the office is that a new partner is going to be named any day now. I already know it's going to be you. You've won more cases than anyone in the past year. I can see it now. Anderson, Moore and Richards. That's got a really nice ring to it!"

"It does, doesn't it?" Mina replied, spinning around in her chair. Just when she grabbed hold of her desk, Mitchell's assistant Abigail appeared in the doorway.

"I'm sorry to interrupt, ladies, but Stephen and Mitchell are asking everyone to meet them in the conference room."

Mina swiveled toward the doorway so fast that she almost fell out of her seat. “Right now?”

“Right now.”

“Why? What’s going on?”

Abigail stepped inside the office. “Apparently they’re planning on naming a new partner very soon,” she whispered. “So they want to make sure everybody’s on top of their game and putting in their best efforts. That’s all I can say, and you didn’t hear it from me!” She gave Mina a knowing wink then rushed out the door.

Karen reached across the desk and grabbed Mina’s hand. “Did you see that wink? The partnership is yours, girl. It’s just a matter of time. I wouldn’t be surprised if they named you partner at this meeting!”

“Now *that* would be phenomenal,” Mina said, giving her hand a squeeze. She shuffled through a pile of papers on her desk and pulled out a notebook, then stood up and smoothed her black pencil skirt over her slim hips. “Shall we go find out what’s going on?”

“Yes. We shall,” Karen said before following her out the door. “Have you prepared your acceptance speech?”

“I’ve run a few ideas through my mind,” Mina joked as the pair entered the conference room.

They each took a seat at the huge cherrywood table, and Mina looked around at her colleagues. Their expressions ranged from curious to anxious. When Stephen and Mitchell entered the room, the entire group turned toward the front and gave them their undivided attention.

"It's showtime," Karen whispered, nudging Mina discreetly.

"Yes, it is." Mina clenched her jaws and folded her hands tightly on top of the table.

"Thank you, everyone, for dropping what you were doing to meet with us," Stephen said. "I'm sure you're all wondering why we've called you here on such short notice."

The group shuffled in their seats while hushed murmurs rippled through the room.

"Long story short," Stephen continued, "We've had several great new developments occur here at the firm during the past year. Interest in our services has increased, new clients are coming onboard, and we're planning to hire more talented individuals such as yourselves to help manage the workload. Now, along with that comes the need for additional leaders to help steer the ship."

Stephen took a step back, and Mitchell stepped forward.

"It's no secret that we're looking to name someone partner," Mitchell said, his right eyebrow shooting up arrogantly toward his hairline. "So with that being said, it's time to start putting your best foot forward, people. Show us what you've got. Give us your all. Convince us that *you're* the one who deserves that honor."

Jeff Stanton, who was Mina's biggest competitor in making partner, pumped his fist in the air. "Heck yeah!" he yelled obnoxiously. "Come on, guys! Let's go!"

"I'm sorry," Karen whispered, "But are we at a basketball

game or a staff meeting?"

Mina suppressed a laugh and kept her eyes glued to the front of the room.

"Loving the enthusiasm, Jeff," Mitchell told him before pointing at everyone around the table. "I think you should all take a page out of his playbook. Get hyped up over this extraordinary opportunity."

"Absolutely," Stephen interjected, "Because it is definitely an unprecedented one. So while Mitch and I are in the process of making a decision on who that new partner will be, just know that we're here to answer any questions you may have. In the meantime, let's get to work, team, and keep winning!"

The group broke out into a round of applause, then chatted excitedly among themselves as they headed out of the room.

Mina looked over at Karen and shrugged. "Oh well. Slow and steady wins the race, right?"

"Right," Karen said quietly, patting her supportively on the back before they returned to Mina's office. "But I just knew that after you won the Colorblind Solutions case, they'd be ready to name you partner *now*. Therefore, due to my disappointment, I think we need to eat the rest of the cupcakes."

Mina laughed and slid the container toward her. "Well I would hate to further exacerbate your trauma, so I concur."

"Thank you for being so understanding of my needs."

Mina picked up the remainder of her own cupcake and shoved it inside her mouth. Just when she reached for another one, there was a knock at the door.

"Come in," she called out.

Stephen cracked the door open and stuck his head inside. "Oh, I'm sorry. I didn't know you were in a meeting."

"No worries," Mina said, quickly brushing crumbs off her blazer. "Would you like a cupcake?"

"No thanks," he said, pointing at his stomach. "I'm watching my ever-expanding waistline. But listen. I'm heading into a meeting with Mitch, and just wanted to stop by and tell you to keep at it. You're doing a great job, and I'm rooting for you."

Mina felt a surge of hopeful energy shoot through her chest. "I absolutely will. Thank you for that."

Stephen nodded his head before closing the door.

"Well that was nice," Karen said right before she swallowed the last bite of her second cupcake. "I just hope that Mitch is on the same page as Stephen. I didn't like that little *sis-boom-bah* moment he had with Jeff during the pep-rally-slash-staff meeting."

Mina rolled her eyes. "You know Jeff is Mitch's little lap dog. He worships the ground Mitch walks on and buddies up to him every chance he gets. I'm just glad to know I've got Stephen on my side."

She glanced down at her watch and saw that it was almost seven o'clock.

"Ooh, I didn't realize it was so late. I need to get going. Calvin and I have reservations that we'll lose if we're not on time."

"Okay, well enjoy yourself. And don't worry. You're going to be named partner any day now."

Mina shut down her computer and grabbed her handbag. "I certainly hope so. Because if Jeff ends up making partner over me, I don't know if I'll be able to work here anymore."

Karen walked with her as they headed toward the lobby. "Look, you're by far the best lawyer at this firm. Everything's going to work in your favor. Trust me."

"Thanks, girl. I'll call you tomorrow."

And with that, Mina hurried to her car and sped off toward Chateau Rocha.

Chapter Two

"A TOAST," CALVIN said, raising his glass as his hazel-specked eyes glimmered with excitement. "To our bright futures as two of the best law partners in California!"

"Correction. *One* of the best law partners that California's ever seen," Mina quipped, a feeling of disappointment stabbing at her chest as she clinked her champagne flute against his.

Calvin shrugged and took a sip from his glass. "Yeah well, you never know, babe. Now that I've made partner at my firm, maybe it wouldn't be such a bad thing if you didn't make partner at yours."

"Why would you say something like that?"

Calvin lowered his eyes and tapped his fingers against the table. "I've been thinking, and…just hear me out. Now that I'm a partner at my firm, I'll be making enough money to take care of an entire family."

Mina slowly set her glass down on the table and glared at Calvin. "Okay, and?"

"Think about it. Maybe Stephen and Mitch not naming you partner at the meeting today was a sign. It could mean that it's time for you to leave the firm altogether so we can start planning our future together. You could stay at home and take care of the household, the children we're planning to have, and—"

"Wait, please. Stop," Mina interrupted, tilting her head to the side in disbelief. "Am I hearing you correctly? Are you actually suggesting that because I didn't make partner today, that I should just quit?"

Calvin smiled at Mina lovingly and reached across the table, taking her hand in his. "I mean, I'm not asking you to quit your job *tomorrow* or anything. But I do think that you'd make a wonderful housewife. And aside from taking care of our home and children, you'd be able to bake as often as your heart desires."

Mina snatched her hand away from Calvin's. "You cannot be serious," she hissed. "Just because I wasn't named partner today doesn't mean I don't want to work anymore."

"Well as far as patent law is concerned, you've been complaining about how bored you are with it for months now. Maybe Stephen and Mitchell did you a favor. Now you can resign and put more effort into our relationship."

"I don't believe this," Mina uttered as her breathing quickened. She reached for her water and saw that her fingers were trembling. "First of all, I wasn't passed over. The announcement just hasn't been made yet."

"You've been giving that firm everything you've got for years. If they wanted you, they would've named you partner by now. And here I am, offering you an opportunity to walk away from a company that doesn't appreciate your talents."

Mina pushed away from the table. "You're offering me an opportunity to walk away and do what? Live a life that was never part of my plan? We've never even discussed me being a housewife." She paused for a moment and scrutinized the sheepish expression on Calvin's face. "Wait, is this about all the other partners at your firm who are married to stay-at-home moms? Are you suddenly trying to fit in with them?"

When he remained silent, Mina stood up. "That's what I thought. And here I was, believing that you were a leader, and *my* partner above all else. I guess I was wrong."

Calvin gripped the edge of the table. "What are you doing? Where are you going?"

"I'm going home. I've suddenly got a pounding headache."

"Mina, please, sit back down. Our entrees haven't even come yet. Maybe you just need to eat and that'll make you feel better."

"No, I just need to go. Congratulations again on making partner."

Before Calvin could say another word, Mina grabbed her handbag and practically ran out of the restaurant.

INSTEAD OF GOING home, Mina decided that she needed to see her parents. She sent her mother a text message on the way to their house, briefing her on all that had happened and letting her know she'd be stopping by.

The minute Mina reached up to ring the bell, her mother Lynn opened the door with outstretched arms.

"Sweetheart, I'm so sorry."

Mina stepped inside the foyer and fell into her mother's embrace. "Thanks, mama," she mumbled into her shoulder.

"Come on. Let's go into the kitchen. We can chat over a hot cup of cocoa."

"Will it be topped with your homemade whipped cream and white chocolate curls?"

"Of course it will. Is there any other way to serve hot cocoa?"

"Nope," Mina said, sighing deeply and wrapping her arm around her mother.

"Well aren't you a sight for sore eyes!" Mina's father Jake boomed. "Come and give your dad a big hug. It's the least I can offer after the rough day you've had."

"Thanks, daddy, I'll gladly take it."

Mina was overcome by a sense of comfort within her father's embrace. When her mother placed a mug filled with hot chocolate in front of her, she took a long sip of the sweet drink, relishing in its soothing warmth.

"Mm, mom, this is delicious. Reminds me of all the hot specialty drinks you served at The Icicle Café."

Lynn glanced over at Jake, who threw her a look. They both turned to Mina.

"Speaking of The Icicle Café," Lynn began, "Your father and I want to talk to you about it."

"But first," Jake chimed in, "If you need to take a minute to vent about what happened with Calvin at dinner, your mother and I are all ears. You should know that I never did like that stuffy, obnoxious little—"

"*Jake*," Lynn snapped through tight lips, "Now is not the time."

"It's okay, mom. I'm fine. I just…I was already feeling a little disappointed that I wasn't named partner today. And when I shared the news with Calvin, he was so dismissive about the whole thing. Then to find out that he doesn't want me working at all…well, that just blew me away. But anyway, enough about that. What's going on with the café?"

Lynn walked over to Jake, and he wrapped his arm around her. "We received a call from the Dawsons today," she said. "Your father spoke with David for what seemed like forever. You know they always have to rehash the same stories they've been telling for years about serving in the military together."

"Of course," Mina snickered before sipping from her mug.

"Then your mother and Betty got going on how The Icicle Café was the best thing that ever happened to Gosberg. They went on and on about their die-hard customers, spectacular recipes and superior customer service. You should've heard them!"

Mina felt her frazzled nerves slowly begin to subside as her parents bantered back and forth, poking fun at one another. The heartwarming conversation was exactly what she needed. But it left her wondering whether she'd ever have a love like that in her life.

"See, dad," she said, "You and Mr. Dawson are good men. While you two were serving your country, you didn't have a problem with your wives branching out and creating careers for themselves. I love that."

"Not that they had much choice in the matter," Lynn retorted. "But seriously, your father and David were extremely supportive of Betty and me. They knew we were two creative businesswomen who had a lot to offer the Gosberg community."

Jake gave Lynn's shoulder an affectionate squeeze. "Absolutely. David and I were proud of our wives, and we were happy to partner with them in order to help make The Icicle Café a huge success."

"That's so awesome," Mina replied before draining her mug. The minute she set it down on the counter, her mother refilled the cup.

"I've had way too much sugar today, mom. But I just can't say no to your hot chocolate."

"I'd be offended if you did."

"So what's going on with the café?" Mina asked. "Are

you all still taking your annual trip to Gosberg this year to check on it and attend The Icicle Fest?"

"We most certainly are," Lynn responded excitedly. She walked over to the oven and pulled out a tray filled with snowflake-shaped sugar cookies. "Betty was telling me about all the wonderful upgrades Scott has made since we were there last year. He's expanded the menu, begun selling winter-themed décor and books, and hosts cooking and crafting workshops on weekends."

"Oh wow. That sounds fantastic. I'm sure the townspeople and tourists are loving it."

"Remember how cute you and Scott were when you two dated back in high school?" Lynn teased.

"Okay, here we go," Mina groaned. "Please, mom, don't start with that. Scott and I dated very briefly. And right after we broke up, he started dating Stacy and I got together with Brandon. So clearly we were better off as friends."

"Yeah, okay, *better off as friends.* All that chemistry between you two told a completely different story."

"I have to agree with your mom there," Jake chimed in. "I always sensed a little something going on between you two well after you broke up."

He reached for a cookie, but quickly snatched his hand away after Lynn swiped it.

"Stop that!" Lynn scolded. "You know those are for tomorrow's creative arts festival down at the veteran's hospital."

"I was only gonna take one," he griped.

"I made a fresh fruit salad earlier today. Why don't you have some of that?"

"Now why would I eat fruit salad when I could be eating one of your famous snowy sugar cookies?"

Lynn rolled her eyes at Jake and turned to Mina. "So anyway, back to Scott. Along with all the upgrades he's made to the café, he is also planning to ramp up this year's Icicle Fest. He's going to throw an even bigger parade, host a ton of new vendors, run several winter-themed contests, and offer up even more good food and music."

"Really?" Mina asked. "That is going to be amazing. I love that Scott has worked so hard to expand the Icicle brand."

Jake cleared his throat. "Yeah…we do, too. He uh…he's probably going to be really disappointed when he finds out we're selling the café."

"Wait, what? So it's official now?" Mina asked.

"Well," Lynn sighed, "David and Betty have decided they're definitely ready to move back to the states. They'd like to free themselves of all business dealings so they can fully enjoy their retirement. So they've asked us if we'd be willing to put The Icicle Café up for sale."

"And what'd you say?"

"We said yes. While your father and I still own half of the café, the Dawsons have really done most of the heavy lifting since we moved to Clover. But in all honesty, each of us has pulled away from a lot of our responsibilities, and Scott's taken them on."

"And he's done a fantastic job," Jake added. "However, I, along with your mother, David, and Betty, am ready to enter the next phase in my life where I don't have to worry about the burden of ownership. We all just want to relax, travel, and do whatever our hearts desire. We've worked hard enough. It's time to let it go."

"Plus," Lynn said, holding her index finger in the air, "Betty has an ulterior motive here. She wants Scott to move back to the states as well so that he can get married and have children. She thinks as long as he's in Gosberg running the café, he'll never have time to find a wife and start a family."

Mina crossed her arms in front of her. "Interesting. Sounds like Betty and Calvin are on the same page with that. I wonder if that's something Scott wants."

"Now that I don't know," Lynn said. "But what I do know is that Betty and David had better break the news to him soon, because they've already found a buyer."

"They have?" Mina asked, surprised to hear that things were moving so fast. "*Wow*. Well, I hope the café is going to a good person who'll take the townspeople into consideration when deciding what to do with it."

Lynn glanced over at Jake. "The café is definitely being purchased by a reputable buyer. But as for the townspeople, I don't know how happy they'll be with the company's plans for it."

"Why not?" Mina asked, noticing that her mother's eyes were tearing up a bit. "Who are you all selling the place to?"

"The Biltmore Corporation," Jake said. "They want to tear down the café and build one of their chain hotels in its place."

Mina's shoulders fell as her eyes darted back and forth between her mother and father. "That kind of sucks, doesn't it? I'm sure the Gosberg community would rather have our beloved café there than some run-of-the-mill hotel, wouldn't they?"

"I'm sure they would," Lynn agreed. "But at this point, we have to go with the offer that works best for us. The Biltmore Corporation is serious, and they're ready to close the deal right after The Icicle Fest. So we have to strike while the iron is hot."

"Understood," Mina said. "As long as you two are happy, I'm happy. And on that note, I'd better get home. I've got a lot to think about. But I really needed this visit. Thank you both for always being there."

"Anytime, honey," Jake said before embracing Mina tightly. "Whatever you decide to do with your life, even if it's dumping Kevin and quitting your job to go train circus animals, we're always going to love and support you."

Mina laughed loudly. "It's Calvin, dad, but you already know that. And thank you for the reassurance. However, no matter how bad it gets, I don't imagine I'll ever train wild animals for a living."

"Ignore your father, dear," Lynn said, wrapping her arm around Mina and walking her to the door. "But since we're on the subject, what do you think you're going to do about Calvin?"

"I don't know, mom. Honestly? I think it's over. He showed me a side of himself tonight that I never knew existed. The selfishness and inconsideration were a complete turnoff. I just can't see myself getting past that."

"Like your father said, we'll support you no matter what you decide. And we're here for you. Love you, hun."

"Love you, too. Keep me posted on the sale of the café."

Mina blew her mother a kiss and headed to her car. The moment she climbed inside, the tears that she'd been holding back ever since she had left the restaurant came streaming down her face.

Chapter Three

KAREN TOOK A sip of her mocha cappuccino while staring across the table at Mina. The pair were sitting out on the patio of the Drink Up Café during a much-needed break from work.

"So let me get this straight," Karen said. "It's over between you and Calvin?"

"Yes."

"Over as in done?"

"Done."

"Finito?"

"Finito."

"*Wow.*" Karen slowly shook her head from side to side while staring up at the sky. "I certainly didn't see this coming. I mean, you two were so good together. A power couple. A dream team. A twosome that I just knew was built to last."

"Yeah, well..." Mina shrugged her shoulders, shaking the ice around in her cup. "I didn't see it coming either. But his newfound vision for our future put the nail in the coffin. There's no way I'd give up working entirely just to sit at home while he's out cultivating his flourishing career."

"At least you've got the partnership to look forward to. So stay the course and keep focusing on that."

"I will. But I don't know how much longer I can keep plugging away at a caseload filled with boring trade secrets and plant patents while the partners take on all the exciting litigations, like new inventions and artists' intellectual property."

"Don't forget you just won the biggest case Anderson & Moore has seen in years. I promise you, your day is coming."

"I hope so…" Mina glanced down at her watch. "We'd better get back to the office. Stephen and Mitchell scheduled a three o'clock meeting with me. Apparently they want to reevaluate my caseload."

"Uh-oh," Karen said, standing up and grabbing her purse. "You know what that means."

Mina's legs felt heavy as she shuffled behind Karen. "Yes. I do. It means they probably want to pass some of their crappy cases off on me so they can spend more time out on the golf course. I'm telling you, something's gotta give."

A stinging feeling of dread attacked Mina's chest when they approached their office building. She pushed through the stiff revolving doors, wondering just what that *something* would be.

LATER THAT EVENING, Mina was at home trying to unwind when her mother called in a complete panic.

"Wait, mom, slow down. What happened, again?"

Mina propped her phone up onto her shoulder and pulled a pumpkin spice Bundt cake from the oven. Between her stove's swirling vent and music playing in the background, she could barely hear what her mother was saying.

"Your father threw out his back!" Lynn yelled. "He can barely move. We're on our way to the hospital now."

"Oh no!" Mina shrieked. "How did he do that?"

"Hold on. I'm going to put you on speaker so that *he* can tell you."

Mina heard her father groaning in the background.

"Hey, honey. *Ow*!" he howled.

"Dad, what happened?"

"I was up on the ladder cleaning out the gutters—"

"After I told him *not* to go up there!" Lynn interjected.

"And on the way down, I slipped past about seven rungs and landed on my back."

"He fell right into the rock garden!" Lynn yelped.

Mina felt her stomach drop as she listened to her parents go back and forth. "Hey, I'm going to meet you all at the hospital. I'm heading out right now."

"No, sweetie," Jake said, his strained tone filled with pain. "You don't have to do that. I'll be fine. I just need to get checked out and pick up some extremely potent pain medication."

"Are you sure? It's no problem at all for me to come down there."

"You've got enough going on," Lynn told her. "Don't worry about your stubborn father who thinks he's still in his twenties. He'll be fine."

"Okay, well, call me as soon as you talk to the doctor."

"We will. Keep your phone close."

"Love you both," Mina said before hanging up the phone. She closed her eyes and rubbed her temples while taking several deep, meditative breaths.

This can't be happening, she said to herself, wondering what else could possibly go wrong.

Earlier that afternoon, she'd felt as though she might burst into flames during her meeting with Stephen and Mitchell. Unbeknown to her, they'd invited Jeff to the meeting as well, making it all the more obvious that she was competing directly with him for the partnership.

Mina sat in stunned silence, watching as Mitchell handed Jeff a slew of interesting intellectual property cases while she was given a stack of dull pharmaceutical disputes. Her jaws clenched as her pile grew higher and higher and Jeff's remained relatively low. But because she was gunning to make partner and prove that she was a team player, Mina took the work on this time, promising herself she'd speak up if it became a pattern.

By the end of the day, all she'd wanted to do was get home and unwind over a nice glass of merlot and an evening of baking. Yet here she was, freaking out over her father's back injury.

Mina turned up the volume on her cell phone so as not to miss hearing her parents' call. She stirred her buttermilk icing one more time then drizzled it over her cake. Just when she cut a slice and sat down on the couch, her phone beeped. She reached for it so quickly that her cake almost slid off the plate.

She expected to see a message from her mother pop up on the screen. But when she tapped the notification, it was a text from Calvin.

Mina smacked her lips and tossed the phone onto the coffee table without opening the message. He was the last person she wanted to hear from.

She turned on the television, and right before shoving a huge chunk of cake inside her mouth, the phone beeped again. This time, it was her mother calling.

"Hey, what's going on?" she asked, struggling not to sound as panicked as she felt.

"The doctor performed a CT scan, and your father has a herniated disc in his lower back. Lucky for him it's not too severe. Some light stretching should help him heal, and he's going to be prescribed ibuprofen."

"I need morphine!" Mina heard Jake wail in the background.

"But the bad news is," Lynn continued, "Your father won't be able to fly to Gosberg next week to check up on the café and attend The Icicle Fest."

Mina exhaled, overcome with relief. "I'm so glad to hear that he didn't hurt himself too badly. And don't worry about visiting Gosberg. I'm sure the Dawsons and the rest of the community will understand that Dad's injury prevented you all from being there."

"That's the thing. We really want our family to be represented at the café and the festival this year. This is the last hurrah before The Icicle Café closes. We'd love to be there to thank the community for all their love and support over the years."

"But mom, you can't go to Gosberg and leave dad here alone. He won't be able to take care of himself."

"You're absolutely right," Lynn responded in a low tone, "which is why we're going to need for you to go in our place."

Mina hopped up off the couch and began pacing the floor. "Wait, *what*?"

"Honey, please, just hear me out. I know you love the café just as much as we do, and I wouldn't feel right if we didn't give the people of Gosberg the proper send-off. They deserve that much, and someone from the Richards family needs to be there. So would you consider doing this for us? We need you."

Mina plopped back down on the couch and pressed her hand against her forehead. "*Mom.* This could not have come at a worse time. I'm in the middle of a battle at work trying to make partner. And I'm still getting over my breakup with Calvin. Trust me. I am in no condition *or* position to go to Gosberg."

"Jake, I'll be right back," Mina heard her mother say.

Here we go... Mina thought, knowing her mother was about to try and sell her on the impossible.

"Sweetie, we're only asking you to go for a few days. You'll arrive in Germany the day before the festival and leave the day after. You'd be back in Clover in no time. And with all that you've got going on, maybe a quick trip back to Gosberg would do you some good. Plus, keep in mind you would be doing this for your family and the beloved town where you grew up."

"You're really pouring it on thick, aren't you?"

"I'm just being honest. Listen to your mother. Get away from the firm for a bit and clear your head. It just may help you put things in perspective. Plus you'll get to reconnect with Scott. You never know. Maybe you two will end up—"

Mina almost choked on her cake. "Please don't start with that, mom. If I do go to Gosberg, it will strictly be for business purposes only."

"Okay, honey. We'll see..."

"Well, I'm glad to hear that dad is okay. Why don't you go check on him? I've got a ton of work to do. Give him a kiss for me and let me know when you all make it home." Mina paused, then fell against the back of the couch. "And I'll start making travel plans."

"That's my girl! Thank you so much for doing this, baby. I know the timing isn't ideal, but hey, maybe something unexpectedly good will come of it."

"Yeah, the Richards will be represented at The Icicle Fest, the café will be sold, the Dawsons can return to the states, and everyone will enjoy their retirement."

"That's not what I was referring to, but I'll let it go. I'd better get back to the room and check on your dad."

"Love you."

"Love you, too."

Mina disconnected the call and opened her laptop. She pulled up the internet, but before logging onto the law firm's website, she opened a search engine and typed in Scott's name. The only sites that appeared were related to The Icicle Café.

"Girl, what are you doing?" Mina asked herself, quickly closing out of the search. But instead of pulling her firm's site back up, she grabbed her phone, tapped an airline app and began pricing flights to Gosberg.

Chapter Four

MINA EXITED THE Munich International Airport and was hit by a blistering gust of wind. She quickly buttoned her wool peacoat and tightened the scarf around her neck. It had been years since she'd actually felt weather that cold. The chilling air penetrated straight through her clothes, right down to her bones.

The trip to Germany had been an unpleasant one, to say the least. It all began when her flight was delayed by over two hours. After she finally boarded, Mina was seated next to a woman holding an overly furry, yapping Maltese who emitted puffs of reeking gas throughout the entire flight. Then the airplane's internet crashed, so Mina wasn't able to get any work done during the entire eleven-hour plane ride.

"These stiletto boots were *not* a good idea," she mumbled to herself through chattering teeth. She struggled to drag her suitcase along the icy sidewalk. As her hair whipped around her face, she squinted her watery eyes and peered up ahead in search of Scott.

"Mina? Is that you?" a deep, distinct voice boomed from behind her.

She spun around and almost slipped at the sight of Scott. Even through the falling snowflakes, Mina could see that he had grown more handsome over time. His penetrating dark brown eyes studied her inquisitively while his full lips formed a faint smile. The frosty temperature cast a rosy glow over his smooth brown skin. And judging from his athletic build, he'd managed to stay in great shape over the years.

"Hey, Scott," she said, tiptoeing over the slippery pavement. "It's been a long time. How are you?"

"Hanging in there. Thanks for asking. Here, let me take that for you."

Scott reached out and grabbed Mina's suitcase. She waited for him to give her a welcoming hug or even a warmer greeting, but neither happened. His unfriendly demeanor appeared more frigid than the temperature.

"My truck is parked pretty close by," he said, pointing up ahead before walking off.

Mina scurried behind him, willing her boots to get her to the vehicle without incident. She was hoping Scott would offer her his arm, but as he walked several steps ahead, it was clear that wasn't going to happen.

When they reached his truck, Scott tossed Mina's suitcase in the backseat and opened the passenger door for her.

"Oh!" she chirped, her tone filled with sarcasm. "How nice of you to get the door. Thank you."

"Don't mention it," Scott retorted. He climbed in the driver's seat, started the engine and sped off without saying another word.

Mina glanced over at him, watching while he stared straight ahead in complete silence. She turned away and looked out the window, her eyes softening at the familiar sight of snow-covered pine trees lining the airport's exit ramp.

"Wow," she breathed. "I forgot how beautiful this place is, especially in the wintertime."

"Yeah, well, that's not surprising considering how long you've been gone."

It suddenly dawned on Mina that Scott wasn't very happy with her visit. But she resisted the urge to reply with an equally snarky comment, refusing to let him get to her.

"Yes, I have been away for quite some time. But in my absence, I heard you've done some really great things with The Icicle Café."

Scott shifted in his seat. "I'd like to think so. But none of that really matters at this point, now does it?"

Mina threw her hands in the air. "Okay, enough with the cynical talk. What's up with you? Why are you acting so cold toward me?"

"Am I acting cold?" he asked, his eyebrows raised in feigned shock. "My apologies. That certainly wasn't my intention."

"Well it certainly appears that way. We haven't seen one another in years, and this is how you treat me?"

Scott grunted and stared out the sideview mirror. Mina

waited for him to respond. When he didn't, she continued.

"Look, I know that what's happening with the café must be hard for you. And you obviously don't want me here. Trust me, I don't really want to be here. But don't worry. As soon as The Icicle Fest is over, I'll be on the first flight back to California."

Mina watched as Scott opened his mouth to speak, then tightened his lips while gripping the steering wheel. After several moments, he finally spoke up.

"I'm surprised you're even staying in town long enough to attend the festival."

"What do you mean? A few days isn't a long time."

"Oh, you'll be here for only a few days? I was under the impression you were coming to town to attend The Icicle Fest."

"I am."

"Well then you're definitely gonna be here longer than a few days. The festival isn't for another two weeks."

"*Two weeks*!" Mina shrieked before throwing her head against the back of the seat. "Oh no. My mother must have gotten the dates mixed up. She thought the festival was happening *this* weekend. I don't know if I can do this..."

"So what are you going to do? Just leave? I know how much it means to your parents to attend The Icicle Fest every year and make sure that your family's presence is felt within the community. It would be nice if you stuck around for it."

"I have a job, Scott. And this is a very pivotal time for me at the firm right now. I don't know if I can swing being away from the office that long."

"Well you came all this way. Maybe you can work remotely until after the festival."

"I don't think that's gonna work," Mina moaned. She pulled out her cell phone and texted her mother, ranting about how she'd given her the wrong festival date.

Scott turned on the radio, and the pair rode in silence while Mina checked her email. By the time she looked back up, Mina realized they had made it into Gosberg and were approaching their high school alma mater. The football team was jogging around the field while punters practiced their kicks on the sideline.

The light turned green and Scott hit the accelerator, driving past the Union Street Park where they used to go sledding and host epic snowball-throwing contests. Children were laying on the ground swinging their arms and legs wildly through the snow in an effort to create the perfect angel. Parents stood around chatting with one another while sipping from their cups of hot cocoa and coffee. Townspeople skated around the ice rink, some performing perfect twirls while other struggled to stay on their feet.

Mina was overcome by a warm feeling of nostalgia. She watched as the people of Gosberg casually went about their day, laughing and talking as if they didn't have a care in the world. She'd forgotten about the sense of calm the town always exuded. It was a feeling that she hadn't experienced in a long time.

"Look at this place," Mina said. "Nothing's changed. It looks great."

"It does, doesn't it?" Scott replied quietly, his tone a bit less hostile.

Mina leaned toward the window as they hit the town's main street and drove past Mindy's Floral Arrangements, Alexandra's Day Spa, and Rarities Antiques and Collectibles. So many fond memories of the times she'd spent hanging out with friends, especially Scott, up and down that strip came rushing back.

"Oh my goodness," Mina said, her eyes tearing up a bit. "Being back here has me feeling all…warm, and fuzzy. Life was so much simpler back in the day. Aside from getting good grades, all we worried about was who had the best jokes, who was hosting the next get together and whether or not our high school football team would win the championship."

"Very true. Life was definitely simpler back then."

When Scott sped past Emma's Bed & Breakfast, Mina held up her hand.

"Hey, wait. Can you turn around? I'm staying at Emma's."

"I know. But your room isn't ready yet."

"How do you know?"

"Because I called and spoke with Emma before picking

you up to find out what time you'd be able to check in. She's booked you in the king suite, and a guest just checked out not too long ago. So you've got about another hour or so until the room is ready."

Mina sat back and slowly crossed her arms, slightly thrown off by Scott's thoughtful gestures. "Oh, okay. Thanks for checking on that for me."

"No problem."

"So where are we going?"

"I was thinking we could stop by The Icicle Café. Thought you might be interested in seeing it after all these years. Maybe order something to eat. I figured you may be hungry after that long flight."

"That actually sounds good. Thank you."

"I also thought that you'd want to stop and change out of those impractical boots. Perhaps put something on that's more appropriate for Gosberg's weather?"

"Ahh, there it is," Mina quipped. "Just when I thought you were being nice, the cynicism in you comes back out."

"What do you mean?" Scott asked, his crooked smile filled with bemusement. "I'm just trying to help you out. Because seriously, what would make you think that wearing those boots—which have the highest heels I've ever seen, by the way—was a good idea in this type of weather?"

Mina rolled her eyes and waved him off. "I really can't wait until we get to the café so that I can get outta this truck."

"Oh, and now you're mad at me because I'm trying to look out for you?"

"Not mad. Just curious as to why you're so worried about what I'm wearing on my feet. It's not like you're really that concerned. If you were, you would've at least helped me to the truck when we were at the airport."

Scott rubbed his forehead sheepishly. "Yeah, I didn't help you out, did I?"

"No. You didn't."

"Sorry about that. I uh…I guess I was a little salty because you haven't been back to visit Gosberg in so many years."

"I'm sorry, Scott. But I've been busy going to law school and working to build my career."

"Just hear me out. I wish you were here in Gosberg to check on the café, or visit with friends. We've all missed you over the years. Every time your parents came to town, I'd expect you to show up with them. But you never did. It seems like after you moved to Cali, you forgot all about us."

Mina felt a slight jab of guilt stab her in the chest. This time, she didn't have a comeback for Scott. Because as much as she hated to admit it, he was right.

When he pulled up in front of The Icicle Café, Mina slowly climbed out of the truck. She stared out at its bright, snow-white brick façade and sparkling picture windows. Scott had maintained the café's cozy, cottage-like exterior beautifully.

The inside glowed like a shining yellow star, and she could see all the employees and customers happily bustling about with their treats and drinks in hand.

Mina once again felt herself tearing up. She pressed the back of her hand against the corners of her eyes as a flood of memories rushed through her mind. From baking with her mother to tasting Scott's experimental dishes to gossiping among her friends, the café housed some of her fondest moments.

She slowly approached the door and dusted snowflakes from the miniature fir trees standing on either side.

"Hey, are you okay?" Scott asked.

"Yeah!" she answered a little too enthusiastically. "I mean…yes. I'm fine."

"Ready to go inside?"

"Yep. Let's do it."

Scott opened the door for her, and when Mina walked inside, she looked around and gasped. Snow-covered tree branches, twinkling lights and shimmering faux icicles hung from the ceiling. The floors were covered in shiny white marble tile. The walls were painted a gorgeous winter white, with glittery silver specks sprinkled throughout. White leather booths lined the walls, and acrylic tables and chairs were scattered around the café. And all of them were filled with customers.

"I cannot believe this place," Mina breathed. "It looks amazing!"

Scott shoved his hands inside his pockets and smiled proudly. "Thank you. I've put a lot of work into it over the years."

"And it shows. You've made so many great changes."

Mina walked over to the bakery counter and admired the festive, winter-themed cookies, cupcakes, donuts and candies.

"I'd like one of everything, please," she joked to the woman standing behind the display.

"One of everything, coming right up!" the woman responded joyfully.

"Mary," Scott said, "I'd like for you to meet Mina Richards. She's the daughter of The Icicle Café's co-owners, Jake and Lynn."

"Oh, Mina! It's so nice to finally meet you!" Mary exclaimed, shuffling around the counter and embracing her tightly. "I've heard so many wonderful things about you. Scott and his parents talk about you nonstop. They're so proud of all your accomplishments. You're a big-time attorney in California, aren't you?"

"Aww, it's so nice to meet you, too. And I don't know about being big time, but I am an attorney, and I do live in California."

"You're just being modest. You are the pride of Gosberg, young lady. And we're so happy to have you here. Are you in town to check out all the cool new upgrades that Scott's made to the café?"

"I am here to check out the café, but I also came in place of my parents since they're unable to attend The Icicle Fest. They really wanted to be here considering this is the last—"

Scott quickly stepped forward and interrupted Mina. "Actually she's uh…she's here to—"

"*Scott*!" someone yelled from the back of the café.

Mina looked over and saw a young, attractive woman standing behind an elaborate all-white coffee bar. Her expression appeared displeased as she eyed Mina from head to toe.

"What's up?" Scott called out.

"Could you please come and take a look at the espresso machine? I can't get the wand to kick out any steam. I think it may be clogged again."

"Ugh, not again," Scott said before pointing at Mina. "Hold that thought," he told her sternly. "I'll be right back."

"Um…*okay*." She watched him curiously while he jogged toward the coffee bar, then turned her attention back to Mary. "So anyway, my parents were planning to be here until my father hurt his back."

"My goodness! How'd he do that?"

"By going against my mother's advice and climbing up on a ladder to clean out the gutters at their house."

"Of course. Typical man!"

"*Basically*," Mina replied before they both burst out laughing. "My mother had to stay back and help take care of him. And that's why I'm here. To represent my folks and give the town a proper send-off before the sale—"

Before she could finish, Scott rushed over and threw his arm around her.

"Hey!" he practically yelled, "You haven't seen the rest of the place yet. Why don't we let Mary get back to work since a line is starting to form around the bakery counter while I give you a tour?"

Mary looked behind her and watched as a large group of people ooh'd and ahh'd while pressing their fingers against the glass.

"Oh, you're right, Scott! I hadn't even noticed. I'd better hop back to it. Mina, it was such a pleasure meeting you," she said, shaking her hand rigorously. "I can't wait to hear all about your life back in California. I bet it's so exciting!"

"I promise you it's not nearly as thrilling as it may seem, but I'd be happy to share. It was nice meeting you as well."

The minute Mary was out of earshot, Mina pulled Scott in close.

"What was that all about?" she asked. "Why are you acting so weird?"

"I'll tell you when we get to a more private area."

"Fine."

He led them toward the coffee bar, which was lined with beautiful shiny silver vintage coffee makers. The menu offered up a variety of hot specialty drinks, from mint mochas to gingerbread lattes, caramel espressos and frozen hot chocolate.

"Everything you serve sounds delicious!" Mina said to the barista who'd asked for Scott's assistance with the espresso machine. Her solemn expression appeared even more dismal than before.

"Hi, I'm Mina," she said with a friendly smile and outstretched hand.

"Hello," the young woman responded dryly before swirling whipped cream into a mug filled with hot chocolate. She topped it off with chocolate powder, grinned brightly and set the mug on top of the counter.

"Jonas!" she called out cheerily. "Your s'mores hot chocolate is ready at the bar!"

Mina stood there in stunned silence as the barista ignored her. She looked over at Scott, who appeared completely oblivious to her rude behavior.

"So," he said, running his hand along the countertop, "This coffee bar is one of our newest additions. And not that The Icicle Café wasn't already the toast of the town, but once we got this component up and running, business completely boomed. Am I right, Lillian?"

"You absolutely are, boss man," she replied, eyeing Scott dreamily while a rosy shade of red slowly spread across her cheeks.

Mina stifled a chuckle at the sight of it, suddenly realizing that the barista was crushing on Scott.

"Lillian," he said, "I'd like for you to meet Mina Richards. She's the daughter of—"

"Of the co-owners, Jake and Lynn Richards," Lillian finished for him without taking her eyes off of Scott. "Yes, I know who she is."

Scott grinned at Lillian, his eyes filled with admiration. "Why am I not surprised?" he asked before turning to Mina. "I'm ashamed to admit that I poached Lillian from a competitor across town, which is where I'd go to get good coffee before we started serving it here. She wouldn't accept the job until she knew everything about The Icicle Café and was sure it'd be a good fit for her."

"And it certainly has been…" Lillian said demurely, slowly wiping down the bar while still eyeing Scott.

"Hm, well, that's nice…" Mina muttered, wanting nothing more than to escape the awkward situation. "The coffee bar is amazing. Why don't you show me the rest of the renovations?"

"I'd be happy to. Follow me."

"Nice meeting you, Lillian," Mina said over her shoulder.

"Likewise," Lillian mumbled.

Scott led her toward what used to be a wall in the back of the café. It'd been knocked down, and an entirely new area had been added. The aesthetic was the same as the eatery, but this section had been transformed into a gift shop. It was filled with winter-themed home décor and trinkets, and shelves that were stacked with festive books and magazines.

"I am absolutely speechless, Scott. You've done such a

phenomenal job with everything. I love it."

"Thank you. That really means a lot coming from you." The shining pride in his eyes dimmed a bit before he continued. "Maybe being back in Gosberg and seeing all this will help you understand why I'm having such a hard time accepting the sale of the café."

"I do understand," she replied softly.

Scott stared at her thoughtfully before his expression brightened. "You know what I think? I think we should sit down over a nice meal and talk. We can catch up, discuss this corporation that's looking to buy the café, and I can share with you a plan I have to keep the café open."

"Hm, well I'm definitely hungry," Mina said, glancing around the gift shop in an effort to deflect from the rest of Scott's suggestions. She had no interest in going against their parents' plan to sell the café so that they could retire.

When her cell phone rang, she immediately dug through her handbag and grabbed it, thankful for the interruption.

"Excuse me one sec," she told Scott before answering the call. "Hello, this is Mina."

"Hi Mina! This is Emma over at the bed and breakfast. Welcome home!"

"Thank you, Emma! It's great to be back. I'm actually over at The Icicle Café now."

Scott waved his hands in Mina's face and shook his head furiously.

"I'm sorry, could you hold on a quick sec?" she asked her

before muting the call.

"What is *wrong* with you?"

He stared down at the floor and whispered, "I haven't told anyone that the café is being sold."

"Wait, you what?"

"I haven't told anyone that the café is being sold. Yet..."

"Why not?"

"Because I just...I couldn't. When people find out, they're going to be heartbroken, and I'm not ready to face that. Plus I'm working to try and find an investor who'll partner with me so that I can hold onto the café."

"Oh, Scott," Mina sighed, wondering what she'd gotten herself into by agreeing to step in for her parents. "Let me get back to Emma. We'll talk about this later."

She stepped away from him and unmuted the call. "Hi, I'm back. Sorry about that."

"No worries. I was calling to let you know that your room is ready."

"Wonderful. Perfect timing. I'll be there shortly."

Mina hung up the phone and turned to Scott. "My room's ready. Would you mind driving me over to Emma's?"

"Of course not. But I thought we were going to sit down, eat and catch up."

She glanced down at her watch. "We were, but...I'd better get going. The internet was down during my entire flight, and I wasn't able to access any of my case files. So that was eleven hours wasted. I've got a ton of work to get done, and considering I'm up for partner, there's no room for me to slack off."

"Okay, well, maybe later," Scott mumbled, his tone filled with disappointment. He followed her through the café and out to his truck. "I wasn't going to take up your entire afternoon, you know," he continued. "Just a quick meal and conversation about the sale."

"I'll tell you what. How about we take a raincheck and reconvene after I get some work done? Would that work for you?"

"Yeah." Scott smiled as he opened the passenger door. "That would definitely work. Hop in. I'll get you over to Emma's so you can get to it."

"Thank you." Mina eyed Scott closely as she climbed inside the truck, convinced that she'd seen a bit of flirtation in his intense gaze.

On the way to Emma's, the pair kept the conversation light while Scott described all the delicious dishes he'd recently added to The Icicle Café's menu. As soon as he pulled into the bed and breakfast's driveway, Emma's husband Charles came bouncing down the stairs.

"Mina!" he boomed when she and Scott climbed out of the truck. "It's so wonderful to see you after all these years. How've you been?"

"Hi, Charles! I've been great, thanks," she said, embracing him warmly. "It's so good to see you, too."

"Emma and I are looking forward to having you. Anything you need, just let us know."

"I really appreciate that. Thank you."

"And isn't this the third time I've seen you today, Scott?" Charles asked him.

"As a matter of fact, it is. But we were more than happy to fulfill your last-minute request and cater Mr. Becker's company retreat."

"What would we have done without you? Old Becker forgot he'd scheduled that event and didn't request the use of our conference room until last night. That's why The Icicle Café is always our go-to when it comes to catering. You never disappoint."

Scott glanced over at Mina before shaking Charles's hand. "That's great to hear, sir. Thank you."

"Most certainly." Charles grabbed Mina's suitcase and headed up the stairs. "I'll meet you at the front desk," he told her. "And no rush. Take your time. I'm sure you two have a lot to catch up on."

"Thanks, Charles," Mina said before turning to Scott. "So The Icicle Café is still the hottest restaurant in town, huh?"

"Of course it is," he replied with a cocky grin. "That's why you need to hear this plan of mine. I'm telling you, Mina. I'm going to do all that I can to keep the café up and running. You know, you should try and stick around longer than a few days. Spend some time at the café and attend a couple of workshops. And you *really* need to check out The

Icicle Fest. It's going to be phenomenal this year."

"I can't guarantee that, but I'll see what I can do."

"Deal," Scott told her before hopping back inside of the truck. "I'll check in with you later to make sure you haven't drowned yourself in legal documents."

"Thanks, I'd appreciate it." Mina laughed, waving as Scott pulled off.

Chapter Five

"IT'S FINE, KAREN," Mina said. She tapped the speakerphone button on her cell phone then ran a flatiron through her hair. "Trust me, I don't have anything to worry about."

She could hear Karen panting frantically through the phone.

"I'm not saying you need to worry, Mina. I'm just concerned after Stephen and Mitch invited Jeff to their country club's annual golf outing. They've never asked anyone from the firm to even visit that pretentious club, let alone attend their sacred golf event."

"And yet I'm still unbothered," Mina said as she spritzed her hair with glossifier. "Because while Jeff is out there schmoozing and drinking and undoubtedly making a fool of himself, I'll be busy researching my new cases and consulting with clients."

"Okay, well…good. I like where your head's at. If you're not worried, then I'm not worried."

"I'm too busy keeping my eye on the prize to be worried. I have got to make partner so that I'll have the power to diversify my caseload. Because if I'm assigned one more plant patent case..."

"Believe me, I'm looking forward to you making partner, too. Don't forget I'm the one who has to help you conduct all your research and draft your documents. But at least the case we're working on now about the hearing aids patent infringement is pretty interesting."

"Eh, I guess."

"Well anyway, how are things going in Gosberg?"

Mina leaned into the mirror and applied a sheer coat of pink lip gloss. "Things in Gosberg have been interesting, to say the least. It's been nice seeing Scott and some of our old hangout spots. And The Icicle Café looks amazing. But Scott hasn't told any of the townspeople that the café is being sold yet. Apparently, he's got some sort of plan up his sleeve to try and keep it open."

"But wait, haven't your parents already found a buyer?"

"Yes. They have. Which is why it's so ridiculous that he has yet to announce the news. People adore The Icicle Café. Scott should've given them fair warning as soon as he found out, because the buyer wants to tear it down and begin construction on a hotel as soon as they close the deal."

"Oh wow. That doesn't sound good."

"It isn't good. And what's worse is that my mother got the dates mixed up for The Icicle Fest. It's not for another two weeks."

"*Two weeks*?" Karen exclaimed. "Hmph. Too bad you're

going to have to miss it."

"Well..."

"Well what?"

Mina took a deep breath as she swiped blush across her cheekbones. "I was actually thinking about working remotely from here until after the festival is over since my parents really want the family to be represented at the event. Plus this is the last fest that the town is ever going to experience, and—"

"*Mina*," Karen interrupted, "you cannot stay in Gosberg for two whole weeks. This is such a vital time for you here at the firm. I'd hate to see you lose that partnership because your presence isn't felt here in the office, *especially* considering how hard frat boy Jeff is gunning for the position."

"Karen. Relax. I got this. I've been killing all of my cases, and Stephen basically told me that the partnership is mine. So don't worry. Plus I haven't even decided whether or not I'm going to stay here."

"Well I hope you decide against it."

Mina's phone vibrated, and a text message from Scott popped up on the screen.

"Hold on a sec. That's Scott texting me now."

Good morning, his message read. *I hope you slept well and got a good amount of work done. Would you like to take a break and stop by the café for breakfast?*

"Ooh," Karen breathed, "so Icicle Café talk aside, what's the vibe like between you and Scott?"

"It's cool. We really haven't had a chance to spend much

time together."

"Mm hm. I can't wait to hear how things go during this little visit," Karen murmured.

Mina giggled at the sound of her sultry tone. "Now you sound like my mother. Just like I told her, I'm here for business purposes only. And on that note, I'd better go. I'm going to meet up with Scott at the café for breakfast."

"Nice. Well, have fun with your new man, and keep me posted on whether or not you decide to extend your visit."

"I'm ignoring you," Mina told her as she slipped on her boots and coat. "But I will keep you posted on my plans. And if anything comes up at the firm, please let me know."

"You got it. Don't forget to email me the final report on the Perfect Pitch Hearing Aids' infringement lawsuit. If Stephen and Mitch ask for it, we've got to be ready."

"I'm on it. Chat soon."

Mina disconnected the call, sent Scott a text message letting him know she'd love to meet him at the café for breakfast, then headed down to the lobby.

"THANKS FOR THE ride, Charles," Mina said when he pulled in front of The Icicle Café.

"It's my pleasure. Emma and I will probably stop by this afternoon for lunch. See you then?"

"Sounds good."

Mina hurried out of the car and inside the café. As soon as she walked through the door, the sweet smell of cinnamon and savory scent of bacon filled her nostrils.

"Good morning, Mina!" Mary boomed. She waved a pair of tongs at her before grabbing hold of a gingerbread man cookie and placing it inside the display case. "Welcome back!"

"Good morning, Mary. It smells delicious in here."

"I hope you brought your appetite with you."

"I did," Mina replied, gripping her stomach as it grumbled with hunger. "I'm actually starving."

"Good. Then you're going to love today's breakfast special. Cinnamon sweet roll French toast with a side of crispy bacon. Would you like to try it?"

"I'd love to. That sounds heavenly."

"I'll put in that order for you right now. And Scott's already got a table set up for you two in the back."

"Perfect. Thank you so much. I'm gonna go and grab one of those tasty specialty drinks from the coffee bar."

"Whatever you choose, trust me, you'll love it."

"I'm sure I will," Mina said, heading toward the back. On the way there, she saw Scott sipping from a mug while Lillian leaned against the counter, swaying back and forth while hanging onto his every word.

Here we go, Mina thought before approaching the pair.

"Good morning, you two," she said cheerily in an attempt to set a pleasant tone.

"Hey, good morning," Scott replied. Lillian mumbled an inaudible greeting, barely looking her way.

"So, are you hungry?" Scott asked Mina.

"I am. I worked so late last night that I skipped dinner. By the time I realized I hadn't eaten, Emma had already shut down the kitchen."

"You should've called me. I would have brought you—"

"Would you like to place an order?" Lillian asked Mina before Scott could finish his sentence.

Mina paused, then turned to Lillian and smiled sweetly.

"Yes. I would. May I please have an eggnog latte?"

"Yes, you may."

"Thanks, Lillian," Scott told her. "Mina and I are going to take a seat over at the corner table. If you wouldn't mind bringing that latte over when it's ready, that'd be great."

"I'd be happy to," she gushed before smiling sweetly at him.

"Thanks," Mina said, resisting the urge to roll her eyes as she followed Scott to the table.

He pulled out her chair, and the minute they sat down, Mary brought over two breakfast specials.

"Mm, this looks amazing," Mina said.

"I certainly can't take credit for it," Mary told her before winking at Scott. "Your friend here recently added this dish to the rotation of breakfast specials, and it's quickly become one of our most popular. I didn't mention this when you first came in, but Scott made sure to set two plates aside so that you could try it before they sold out."

"Oh, did he now? Why am I so surprised to hear that?"

"Where's the discretion, Mary?" Scott asked her through a sheepish grin. "You're willing to break the trust between you and I for someone you just met yesterday?"

"Come on. Mina is practically family. We don't have to keep secrets from her."

Mina giggled at the pair's heartwarming banter. But her laughter faded when she thought about how Scott had yet to tell Mary that the café was being sold, and how Mary would lose a job she clearly adored.

Lillian approached the table and cleared her throat. "Here are your lattes," she said before setting them down.

"Oh, I didn't order one, but thank you," Scott told her. "That was very thoughtful."

"Of course. You're so welcome."

Mina opened her mouth to say thank you, but Lillian rushed off before she had the chance.

"Okay," Mary said, patting their shoulders, "I'll let you two enjoy your breakfast."

"Thanks," Mina said as she drizzled warm maple syrup over her French toast then took a bite. "*Scott*, this is crazy good!"

"Glad you like it. This dish sells out really fast whenever it's on the menu."

"So why don't you make it a permanent option?"

Scott shrugged his shoulders. "I've been considering it.

But what would be the point if the café is sold?"

Mina stopped chewing and looked across the table. He stared back at her, his soft expression filled with both sadness and hope.

"So you say you've got a plan to try and keep this place in business," Mina told him. "Let's hear it."

Scott's mood suddenly appeared to lift as he bit into a piece of bacon and sat up straighter in his chair. "Okay, check this out. There's a potential investor named Felix who runs a chain of family-owned restaurants in Munich. He just so happened to be passing through Gosberg a few months ago and stopped by the café with his wife and twin daughters. The entire family loved the concept of this place and flipped out over the food."

"No surprise there," Mina interjected. "Both the café and the food are amazing."

"Thank you. I can tell you love it, too, because you're over there tearing up that French toast."

Mina picked up a piece of bacon and acted as if she was going to throw it at him. "Will you stop it and finish telling me about Felix!"

"Okay, okay," Scott laughed after quickly ducking to the side. "So anyway, when I found out our parents had decided to sell the café, I immediately called Felix and explained the situation. I asked if he'd be interested in partnering with me since he understands the dynamics of a family-owned business, appreciates what The Icicle Café means to the

Gosberg community, and respects my passion for this place."

"Well he certainly sounds like a great partner to have. What'd he say?"

"He mentioned how much of a commitment it would be, and that he's never worked with anyone outside of his own family. So partnering with me would completely take him out of his comfort zone. But Felix does love what I'm doing with the Icicle brand and sees its huge potential for growth. In the end, he asked if I could give him some time to think about it."

"And what did you tell him?"

"Of course I told him yes. Ultimately, I think he'll be willing to invest. It's just going to take a little convincing."

"The clock is ticking, Scott. The Biltmore Corporation is planning to close on the café right after The Icicle Fest. What's it going to take for you to talk Felix into partnering with you?" Mina asked before shoving another forkful of French toast inside her mouth and savoring the sweet, gooey goodness.

"Honestly? I think that The Icicle Fest is all it'll take to seal the deal. I've already invited him and his family to the event. Once he sees how spectacular it is and realizes just how much the festival and café mean to the Gosberg community, he'll be eager to partner with me."

Mina sighed while swirling her latte around in the cup. "I don't know. As far as your timeline is concerned, you're cutting it awfully close. But…I have faith in you. I think you can pull it off."

"Thank you. I appreciate that. And I have faith in you, too. Because once Felix meets you and understands that your family is such a huge part of The Icicle Café's success story, I *know* he'll be ready to go into business with me."

Mina took a sip of her drink while peering over the rim of her mug at Scott. "You are not slick, sir. I have yet to confirm that I'll be staying in town for The Icicle Fest."

"Come on, Mimi! I need you. I need your charisma and charm, and that ability to hit Felix with the litigation skills that'll sway his decision in my favor."

"Wow," she laughed while shaking her head. "I just had a flashback of us during high school, sitting in this café while you harassed me about one thing or another. Some things never change."

"But some things do. A lot changed when you quit me during our junior year and started for Brandon, then abandoned me after graduation for the greener pastures of California."

"First of all, please stop rewriting history. You quit me for Stacy."

"Stacy who?" Scott asked before he and Mina both burst out laughing.

"I see you've suddenly come down with a case of selective amnesia," Mina said. "That's cute. But seriously, I'll have to play things by ear as far as staying in town is concerned. I need to see what's going on at the law firm before I commit to anything."

"Fair enough." Scott sat back and folded his arms. "So it sounds like things are going really well for you with your career."

"They are. They'll be even better once I'm named partner."

"Okay," Scott said while slowly nodding his head. "I'm happy for you, Mina. And proud. You've always worked hard for what you want. It's nice to see that everything is paying off."

"Thank you. I can say the same for you, too. What you've done with The Icicle Café is phenomenal."

"I appreciate that. Let's just hope I can hold onto it."

Mina drained her mug then cleared her throat. "So…do you think you should tell the employees and townspeople that the café might be sold? Because what if things with Felix don't work out? I'd hate for them to find out when the demolition trucks pull up and start tearing the place down."

"I'm honestly not even thinking along those lines. I am confident that Felix is going to come on board after he attends The Icicle Fest."

Mina's cell phone buzzed before she could respond. She glanced down and saw a text from Karen pop up on the screen.

"Excuse me for one second," she said before tapping the message.

EMERGENCY! Stephen and Mitch just told me they need the Pitch Perfect report ASAP. Apparently the president of the compa-

ny wants to file the lawsuit with the court immediately. How soon can you send it?

"Ugh, I knew I should've brought my laptop with me," Mina said.

"Why, what's going on?"

"I have a report that I need to send to the partners at my law firm. Would you mind dropping me back off at Emma's?"

"Of course not."

Mina wrote Karen back letting her know she'd send it soon, then took a few more bites of food.

"You ready?" she asked Scott.

"I'm ready. Let's go."

The pair headed to the front of the café. Mina stopped at the bakery counter, where Mary was busy filling out the chalkboard menu.

"Thanks again, Mary," she said. "I'll see you later."

"Oh, you're welcome, honey. Will you be back tonight for dinner? Scott's serving up his famous fried bratwurst and potato salad. From the sound of things, the entire town is coming in for it."

"I'll try my best. I've got a ton of work to do."

"I hope you can make it!" Mary said before turning back to the chalkboard and adding the cupcake flavors of the week.

"Aww, no red velvet cupcakes while I'm in town?" Mina asked.

"We actually don't serve red velvet cupcakes," Mary told

her.

"*Huh*?" Mina turned to Scott. "But The Icicle Café is famous for my mother's red velvet cupcakes. What happened?"

"Well for starters, your mother moved to California," he said. "And as hard as everyone has tried, no one's been able to replicate her recipe. So we ended up having to take them off of the menu."

Mina tapped her finger against her chin, then reached down and pulled a red piece of chalk from the box.

"Here," she said, handing it to Mary. "Add red velvet cupcakes to the menu."

"Why would we do that?" Scott asked.

"Because I'm going to bake a few batches for the café today."

"*Really*?" he asked, his eyes wide with shock. "Why would you do that?"

"Because this town deserves to experience my mother's cupcakes. And they just so happen to be my specialty. So here's the plan. I'm going to write up a grocery list, and if you wouldn't mind picking up the ingredients, I'll bake them to go along with tonight's dinner special."

"Seriously?" Scott asked, his huge grin practically covering his entire face.

"Yes. I'd be happy to. But if we're gonna make that happen, I need to get back to the bed and breakfast and get to work on my report."

"All right then, let's go."

"I can't wait to try those cupcakes," Mary said, frantically clapping her hands as Mina and Scott rushed out the door. "See you tonight!"

On the way back to Emma's, Mina typed out a grocery list on her phone and texted it to Scott.

"I just sent you the ingredients I'll need for tonight. Thanks again for picking them up. I'd go with you if I didn't have to get this report done."

"It's no problem. I'm actually surprised you're doing this. I mean, I'm really happy about it, but I didn't think you'd have time."

"Maybe being back in Gosberg and spending time at the café has inspired me. Plus you know I love to bake. It's actually a great stress reliever for me."

"Well I'm really glad to hear that, and I'm excited to try your cupcakes," Scott told her as he pulled in front of Emma's. He hopped out and opened the passenger door. The pair locked eyes, and Mina felt a slight twinge in her chest at the sight of his crooked smile.

"Thanks for the ride," she told him before stepping out of the truck. "Can you pick me back up at about four? That should give me enough time to bake several batches of cupcakes before dinnertime."

"Four sounds good. See you then."

"See you then."

Mina bounced up the stairs and inside the lobby. When

the door closed behind her, she turned around and saw that Scott was still standing in the driveway watching her. She waved goodbye, then hurried up to her room.

Chapter Six

MINA STOOD BEHIND the bakery counter at The Icicle Café, watching as a group of Gosberg High students headed toward the door.

"Thanks again for the cupcakes, Mina!" one of the girls called out. "They were sooo good!"

"You're welcome! Glad you enjoyed them."

"We hope you add them to the regular menu, Scott!" one of the guys said on the way out.

"I'll see what I can do," he replied.

Mina threw Scott a look before handing several empty cupcake pans to a busboy.

"Stop it with the faces," Scott told her. "I know what that look means. Don't worry. I'll let everyone know what's going on in due time."

"Whatever you say, my friend. Just remember, the clock is ticking."

"I know, I know. But for tonight, can we just enjoy the fact that we had one of the most successful evenings that The Icicle Café has seen in months?"

"We most certainly did," Mary said, rushing toward the

bakery counter. "Mina, can you toss a couple of red velvet cupcakes in a to-go bag for me?"

"I sure can. Hey, Scott? I wish I could stay longer, but I really need to get back to Emma's. Would you mind dropping me off?"

"Of course not. Mary, can you hold down the fort until I get back?"

"Absolutely."

"Thanks, Mary," Mina said, handing her the bag of cupcakes. "I had such a good time working with you tonight."

"Likewise. Will you be back tomorrow?"

"At the rate I'm going, probably."

"Good! See you then."

Mary hurried off with the cupcakes, and Mina glanced around the café before turning to Scott.

"Tonight was just like old times, wasn't it?"

"It sure was. And we still make a great team," he said before giving her a high-five.

"Yes, we do. And now, back to reality. I'd better get you back to Emma's so that you can get to work on your *other* job."

"That would be nice, thanks," Mina said on the way out the door.

When the pair arrived at the bed and breakfast, she looked out at the twinkling lights hanging from snow-covered tree branches that illuminated the cobblestone driveway. She took a deep breath, and a button popped open on her coat.

"Uh-oh," she said before bursting out laughing.

"What's wrong?"

"I'm literally busting out of my coat. I should not have let you talk me into that second helping of bratwurst."

"Uh-uh. Nope. I am not about to let you rewrite history and put that blame on me. You were the one who insisted on a second helping."

"And you and Mary were happy to oblige."

Scott nodded his head in agreement. "Now that I can't deny."

"And as an attorney, I'm here to tell you that the court finds you guilty as charged."

"On what grounds?"

"You were a willing accomplice."

Scott threw his hands in the air. "All right. You got me. I always knew you were a fantastic baker, but who knew you'd end up being such an amazing lawyer as well?"

"Aww, thank you."

"Wait," he continued, "Let me expound upon that. I figured you'd be a great attorney too, because that's all you talked about throughout elementary and high school. And you dressed up as a lawyer every year for Halloween."

Mina threw her head back and covered her mouth. "Yes! I did, didn't I? Wow. I forgot all about that."

"I didn't..."

The twosome fell silent. Scott's gaze fell from Mina's

eyes down to her lips. She quickly stared down at her hands, which were folded tightly in her lap.

"So uh…Thanks again for tonight," he told her. "Those cupcakes of yours were the hit of the evening. We've never had a dessert fly off the shelves that fast."

"Aw, that's really flattering. I'm just glad everybody enjoyed them." Mina glanced at her cell phone and checked the time. "I should go. I haven't opened my email in hours."

"Hey, what are you doing tomorrow?"

"I've got a video conference call with the law firm in the morning. Then it's back to working on my caseload. Why? What's up?"

"I was thinking we could hang out at Union Street Park and take a spin around the ice skating rink. Or maybe throw a few snowballs. You know, for old time's sake."

Mina contemplated the laundry list of assignments she needed to get done for work. As she mentally debated whether or not she'd have time to hang out with Scott, he reached over and gave her hand a slight squeeze.

"Come on. All that work isn't going anywhere. It's been years since you've visited Gosberg, and you'll be leaving before you know it. Have some fun while you're here. Let's visit a few of our old spots and catch up with one another. What do you say?"

Mina felt her heartbeat speed up as the warmth from Scott's skin penetrated hers. "If I get enough work done tonight and tomorrow morning, then I'll try and sneak away for a bit."

"Okay cool," he said, breaking out into an elated grin. "I'll check in with you in the morning. Maybe I can also bribe you into coming by the café for a specially prepared lunch in exchange for more of those red velvet cupcakes."

"We'll see," Mina replied coyly, reaching down and grabbing her handbag. "But you should know that those cupcakes aren't my only specialty. They're just the tip of the iceberg when it comes to my baking repertoire."

"Are they really? Please, tell me more."

"Come on now. I can't reveal all of my trade secrets at once. But if you're willing to whip up a specially made lunch just for me, maybe I'll bake a few batches of my highly requested blizzard brownies."

"My mouth is already watering...Okay, it's a date."

A date, Mina thought to herself as she stepped out of the truck. Before she had a chance to overanalyze Scott's comment, her cell phone rang.

"I need to take this. It's Karen. Talk to you tomorrow?"

"Yes, you will."

Mina closed the door and hurried up the stairs, rushing to get out of the cold. She turned and waved at Scott, who waited until she had made it inside before pulling off.

"Hey girl, perfect timing!" she said after picking up the call. "I just got in from The Icicle Café. We had such a fun night. I actually baked a few batches of my red velvet cupcakes, and the customers *loved* them. It really felt good to—"

"Mina, listen," Karen interrupted, her voice filled with panic. "We've got a situation. Have you checked your email?"

Mina felt her heart drop down to her stomach. "No. I was just heading up to my room to check it now. What's going on?"

"Stephen and Mitch reviewed the potential arguments you submitted in response to the Pitch Perfect Hearing Aids infringement case. They don't think they're strong enough to protect the company's patent against the defendant in court."

Mina leaned against the wall and pressed her hand against her palpitating chest. "Okay. Well, uh…I can fix that. I'll just reevaluate the technical features of Pitch Perfect's patent and come up with assertions that further validate the—"

"Hold on," Karen interjected. "You don't have to do all that. Because unfortunately…the partners reassigned the case to Jeff."

"*What*? Wait…why? How come no one called to discuss this with me first before making such a huge move?"

"Mina, they tried. Several times. But the calls wouldn't go through. That's why I emailed you high priority hours ago. When the partners didn't hear back, they had no choice but to move on. Pitch Perfect's trial is set to begin next week, and the company execs were anxious to hear our game plan."

Mina's eyes burned with tears. "I cannot believe this,"

she whispered. "So was Jeff able to come up with something that the partners approved of?"

"Yes," Karen replied sullenly.

"Oh really? What?"

"I don't know how he did it, but the man somehow managed to review the entire case file and present a really persuasive list of claims against the defendant. Stephen and Mitch loved it, and so did the president of Pitch Perfect."

Mina cradled her head in her hand and willed herself not to cry. "This is a disaster. I need to get back to Clover. Immediately."

"Yes, you do. Any news on when the closing is going to happen?"

"No. And if it doesn't happen soon, they're going to have to postpone it altogether until my father's well enough to fly here and sign the papers himself."

"Well in the meantime, let's stay positive and move on to your next case. We'll knock that one out the park and keep you on track to becoming partner."

"I'm still trying to wrap my head around the fact that Stephen and Mitch just handed Pitch Perfect over to Jeff."

"Listen, try not to take it personal. The company's new hearing aid devices are set to hit shelves next month, and they didn't have much time to spare. I don't think this one little glitch is going to affect your chances."

"I would love to hear that from Stephen and Mitch during our video call tomorrow."

"Oh, wait," Karen said, "I forgot to mention they canceled the call now that Jeff has taken over the case."

A rumbling wave of nausea hit Mina square in the stomach. "This is not good…"

"Uh-uh, don't do that. Keep your head up and let's remain optimistic. Like I said, we'll get 'em next time."

"Okay. I need to go process all of this. I'll call you tomorrow."

Mina hung up and dragged herself to her room. As soon as she fell onto the bed, her phone buzzed. It was a text from Scott.

Thank you again for such a great night. I am beyond impressed at how much of a huge hit both you and your cupcakes were. Can't wait for you to kill it with the brownies tomorrow. Don't work too hard tonight…

"That's the problem," she said aloud while responding to his message. "Apparently I haven't been working hard enough."

Thanks, Scott. I had a really good time, too. But unfortunately, I'm not going to be able to make it tomorrow, she wrote. *Some things came up at work that I need to tend to.*

Mina sent the text then tossed her phone across the bed.

"Get your head in the game, girl," she told herself before grabbing her laptop, opening the Henderson Analytics case folder and delving into their patent application.

Chapter Seven

MINA HELD HER arms up over her head and spun around quickly. When she managed to stay on her feet instead of landing on her backside, she clapped her hands loudly.

"Woo hoo!" she yelped. "Did you see that?"

"I did!" Scott said as he skated toward her. "Looks like you still got it, Richards."

"Back like I never left."

Mina had stayed up well into the night working on her Henderson Analytics patent litigation strategy. She'd emailed it to Stephen and Mitchell as soon as it was done the next morning and was surprised when they responded within an hour. Both partners loved her plan and even apologized for having to pass the Perfect Pitch case on to Jeff. Either way, Mina was happy to be back in their good graces. So happy that she'd even let Scott convince her to go ice skating that afternoon.

"Aren't you glad I talked you into coming out and getting some fresh air?" he asked.

"You know, I am actually. Things were pretty hectic with

work last night, but I got a nice little win today, so I'm considering this outing a celebration of sorts."

"A celebration? Nice. I'm flattered." Scott skated closer toward her. "So, patent law. That must really be your passion, huh?"

"That's an interesting question. And one that I seem to keep asking myself more and more these days."

"That can't be good, can it?"

"I think this conversation is going to require a cup of hot chocolate. Topped with extra marshmallows."

"Is it really?" Scott asked, smiling at her affectionately. "Okay then. Two hot chocolates, coming right up."

The pair skated over to the rink's igloo-shaped snack shack and bought their drinks, then took a seat on a nearby bench. Mina sipped her cocoa and turned to Scott.

"So, back to your question about whether I'm passionate about patent law. When I first started out, it seemed really exciting. I loved the idea of working with enthusiastic inventors on their creations, and helping artists and musicians protect their intellectual property."

"Remember how you used to brag about becoming Janet Jackson's personal attorney and copyrighting all her music for her?" Scott asked.

"Ha! I do remember that. And I'm still waiting for the opportunity to present itself. But as far as the work is concerned, it can be a bit tedious at times, and mundane. That's why I'm working so hard to become partner."

"Would that change things for you? Becoming partner?"

"It could. I mean, along with the perks of earning a higher salary and acquiring equity stake in the firm, I'd have more say in which cases I'm assigned. That alone could help reignite my passion. Because in all honesty, it's dwindled over the years."

"Hm," Scott murmured curiously. "Do you ever wonder whether you're trying to force something that's no longer there?"

Mina looked away from him and stared out at the rink. "I've never really thought about it that way considering how hard I've worked to get where I am today." She took a long sip of hot chocolate. "What about you?" she asked, eager to change the subject. "Seems like your love for cooking and the café are stronger than they've ever been."

"Oh yeah, definitely. I love creating new recipes and bringing joy to my customers through food. Then once our parents asked me to oversee the café, that was it. I was bitten by the entrepreneurial bug and implemented all the new additions, created the Icicle Fest, and started hosting the cooking and crafting workshops."

"It's really fantastic how you've expanded the Icicle brand. And just think, all those wonderful ideas were born from a little eatery that our parents built back when we were kids."

"Yes they were. And what I've done so far was just the tip of the iceberg. I had so many more plans and ideas that I was working to develop. But now..."

When Scott's voice trailed off, Mina looked over and saw that his elated expression had fallen. He stared straight ahead blankly. His lips were parted as if he wanted to say more, but he didn't. She searched for the right words that would offer some sort of consolation, but couldn't come up with anything.

Scott quickly swiped his hand over his eyes and glanced down at his watch. "It's already three o'clock? I didn't realize it had gotten so late."

"Time flies when you're having fun. Isn't that what they say?"

"Yes. And it's the truth, because I'm definitely enjoying myself."

The pair held a stare that lasted several seconds. Despite the chilly wind, Mina felt her cheeks beginning to burn. She loosened the scarf around her neck and stood up.

"Hey, why don't we head over to the café?" she asked. "I haven't eaten since breakfast, and all I had was a cranberry muffin and fruit. Maybe we could have a late lunch, then I can bake a few batches of those blizzard brownies that I promised you."

Scott hopped up. "I'm glad you mentioned that, because when I told Mary about the brownies, she did a little happy dance and added them to the chalkboard along with tonight's dinner special."

"Did she really? Well thank goodness I was able to get all

my work done. Not to mention I'm willing to pitch in at the café and for free work!" she joked before nudging Scott playfully.

He grabbed her hand, and together they bladed toward the rental booth to return their skates before heading off to The Icicle Café.

"YOU DID IT again, Mina," Mary said, taking a bite out of a warm brownie fresh from the oven. "These are sinfully delicious. The marshmallows are melting into the chocolate chips, the caramel is oozing everywhere…they're perfection."

"Thanks, Mary. It looks like this last batch is going to sell out within the next few minutes," Mina told her as she handed a bag of brownies to Mrs. Weber. "Thank you so much! I hope you enjoy them."

"Oh, these aren't for me," Mrs. Weber replied. "I'm taking them home to my husband and kids. I already ate two while dining with my book club. And I should feel guilty, but I don't."

"Good," Mina said. "You shouldn't."

"This is my second helping," Mary chimed in, "And I don't feel guilty either!"

"Glad I'm not alone in my thinking," Mrs. Weber said with a wink. "See you ladies tomorrow!"

"Have a good night!" Mary said before whispering to

Mina, "Do you hear all this great feedback you're getting? And look at the long line of customers!"

Mina peered around the corner and saw that the bakery line was practically out the door.

"This is all so unbelievable. And unexpected. I never thought I'd be back in Gosberg baking at the café. Quite honestly, it feels really good to prepare my favorite desserts for everyone and hear how much they love them."

"It should. If you ask me, this is your calling. Your heart seems so full whenever you're here, baking and interacting with the customers. Have you ever considered moving back to town and working at the café?"

Mina's mood dampened a bit at the thought of Mary not knowing that the café might be closing. "Oh no," she told her. "I'm really invested in my law career, and I love living in California."

"Uh-huh," Mary muttered while ringing up an order. As she waited for the credit card to process, she propped her hand on her hip. "What about all that talk I heard earlier today about patent law being dull, and how some frat boy at your firm snatched a case right from underneath you?"

"Well, that's why I'm working so hard to make partner. The more power I have, the more control I have over my caseload, the way I'm treated..."

"Sounds too cutthroat for me. I'd rather work in an upbeat, pleasant environment in a cozy small town, where everybody knows everybody's name and we all look out for one another. All that corporate, big city living just seems so unappealing."

Mina slowed down while stacking brownies inside a bag as Mary's words resonated in her mind. "I guess I can see your point." She handed the bag to Lea, a teenager who worked at the ice skating rink's snack shack.

"Here you go. I hope you enjoy them."

"I already did." Lea giggled. "I ate mine and half of my brother's after dinner. These are for tomorrow. Did you know that some of the kids at school are planning to create a petition, demanding that Scott add your red velvet cupcakes and these blizzard brownies to the dessert menu permanently?"

Just as Mina and Mary burst out laughing, Scott walked over.

"A petition, huh?" he asked. "Couldn't you guys have just pulled me to the side and asked nicely? Why make it so official? I'm starting to feel threatened and ganged up on here."

When Scott pressed his hands against his chest defensively, Mina swatted his shoulder with an oven mitt. "Stop being so dramatic. Lea, I'll be sure to leave the recipes with Mary so that once I'm gone, she and Scott can discuss making those items permanent fixtures on the menu."

"Thanks, Mina!"

"No problem," she said before noticing that Scott was staring at her. He moved in closer and whispered in her ear,

"Now why would you go through all that trouble, knowing that the café might be sold? Looks like somebody's becoming convinced that I can hold on to this place..."

Before she could respond, he began backing away.

"Hey Mary," he continued, "We need to get together and brainstorm ideas on this weekend's workshop. See if you can come up with something good that we haven't done yet."

"You got it!"

She and Mina watched while Scott headed over to the coffee bar. Lillian handed him a drink and whispered something in his ear. They both burst out laughing, and she patted his back affectionately.

"That girl is determined to get together with Scott," Mary said. "Ever since he brought her on board, she's been chasing after him. But after *you* arrived, I've noticed she's turned her flirtatious little antics up a notch. I think she feels threatened by you."

"She shouldn't. Because I'm certainly no threat. But uh, does Scott seem to be taking the bait?"

"I don't think so. He's just being nice in an effort to create a warm, friendly atmosphere here in the café. If you ask me," Mary continued, glancing over at Mina slyly, "I think he's got a thing for you. And Lillian is a sweetheart, but I've noticed how she's been giving you the cold shoulder. Maybe she senses he's got feelings for you, too."

Mina waved her off. "I seriously doubt that. Scott and I

are just friends. We dated for a minute in high school, but that didn't last very long. And after I left Gosberg, neither of us made enough effort to stay in touch with one another."

"But obviously the bond that you two have is still there. Which brings me back to a question that you never answered. What really brought you to town, Mina? Are you here to check in on the café, or are you here to check in on *Scooott*?"

Mina giggled and bumped Mary with her hip. "Will you stop with all that! I'm actually here to check on the café."

"What are you two over here whispering about?" Scott asked before stepping around the counter and taking the next order.

"Thanks for coming to help out," Mina said, eluding his question. "We could use some assistance in shortening the line, which seems to be getting longer."

"Could it be because Mary's busy sneaking brownies while you're both gossiping like two schoolgirls?"

"*Possibly*." Mina snorted sarcastically.

Just as Scott opened his mouth to respond, Mr. Klein strolled to the front of the line.

"Tonight's dinner was absolutely delicious, and there are no words to describe those brownies," he said. "I hope you all are planning to add them to the menu permanently."

"We're working on it," Mary told him.

"Good. So have you all figured out the theme of this weekend's workshop? My wife and grandkids are planning to attend, but when they went to the café's website, they said the calendar hadn't been updated."

"We're working on that, too," Scott replied. "There's been so much going on around here, and with Mina coming to town, things have been a bit hectic."

"Tell me about it," Lillian interjected, who'd just delivered a tray of drinks to a nearby table.

"Gir—" Mina began before she caught herself. *Let it go*, she thought, watching through squinted eyes as Lillian walked away. When Mary nudged her arm, Mina turned her attention back to the group.

"Hey," she said, "have you all ever held a gingerbread house workshop?"

All eyes shifted to her.

"No, we haven't," Scott replied, tapping his index finger against his lips thoughtfully.

"That's because no one here really knows how to make gingerbread houses," Mary said. "You should see the pitiful little brown sheds the townspeople put on display during the holidays."

"Be nice, Mary," Scott said. "At least they're trying."

"Well I know how to build fantastic gingerbread houses," Mina said, "Courtesy of my mother, of course. Maybe I could lead the workshop."

"That'd be great!" Mary exclaimed.

"It certainly would," Mr. Klein said. "My wife and grandkids will love that. I don't think they've ever even attempted to build a gingerbread house."

Scott eyed Mina optimistically. "Do you think you'll still be in town this weekend?"

"Oh, wait, I forgot about that," she responded quietly. "Why don't we wait and see how things go?"

"But you have to stay," Mary insisted, practically jumping up and down. "The townspeople would go crazy over a gingerbread house workshop."

"I have to agree with you on that," Scott said. "You know what would be even cooler? *If* Mina stays, we could turn the workshop into a contest. The person with the best gingerbread house could win a personal baking lesson with her."

"Ooh I love it, I love it, I love it!" Mary squealed, throwing her hands in the air. "Mina, you have to stay in town long enough to conduct the workshop. Please do that for us. *Please*?"

Mina looked around at everyone's hopeful expressions. And then, unable to resist, she finally said, "Okay. I will."

"Yes," Scott said, pumping his fist before running around the counter and heading to the front of the restaurant.

"Attention everyone," he called out. "We've just decided the theme of this weekend's workshop. For the first time ever, we are going to teach you how to make a gingerbread house. And by *we*, I mean our resident celebrity guest baker, Mina Richards!"

The crowd broke out into a flurry of cheers. Mina

clutched her hands together and smiled brightly, flattered by their reaction.

And for the first time since arriving in Gosberg, her caseload was the furthest thing from her mind.

Chapter Eight

"YOU'RE NOT COMING home until next week?" Karen screeched. "Come on, Mina! You can't be serious. Especially after Jeff stole your case right from underneath you. What is going on?"

Mina lowered the volume on her video chat. She was sitting inside the conference room at Emma's, surrounded by her laptop, tablet, second cell phone and work binder.

"I'm not going to lie to you, Karen. I got caught up. The Icicle Café was packed last night, and the blizzard brownies that I baked were a huge hit."

"I get it. Congratulations. But what does that have to do with you staying in Gosberg until next week?"

"I promised Scott that I'd conduct the café's workshop this weekend. I'm going to teach the townspeople how to make a gingerbread house. It's gonna be awesome."

Mina watched as Karen dropped her head in her hand.

"I know, I know," Mina said. "It might not seem like a big deal to you. But for a café that was built on a wintery theme, it doesn't make sense that Scott's never hosted a gingerbread house—"

"*Mina,*" Karen interrupted, "You do know that Jeff won the Perfect Pitch case yesterday, don't you?"

Mina watched as Karen's forehead wrinkled with worry. "I do know that. But the good news is, I got great feedback from Stephen and Mitch on the preliminary arguments I submitted on behalf of the Henderson case. And I'll be back in Clover way before it's time to present their case in court."

Karen stared down at her intertwining fingers as her chin began to tremble.

"What wrong?" Mina asked her.

"There's something I haven't told you."

"What?"

"A few of Henderson's top executives came into the firm this morning."

Mina shrugged her shoulders. "Okay, well, it couldn't have been for any official business, because the partners would've included me."

When Karen didn't respond, Mina pressed her fingertips against her forehead. "It wasn't a formal meeting, was it?"

"Yes. It was. But that's not the worst part."

"Really? How much worse could it get?"

"The partners invited Jeff to sit in on the meeting."

Mina jumped up out of her chair and began pacing the floor. "What? But why? What purpose did that serve? Jeff doesn't have anything to do with this case."

Karen inhaled sharply. "I know. But Mitch emailed me late last night and asked that I forward all of the information we've gathered on Henderson to Jeff. So he's obviously trying to loop him in."

Mina froze. She tried to take a breath but felt as though she were being suffocated. She wrapped her hand around the base of her neck and slowly sat back down.

"Are you okay?"

"No. But I will be. I hope..."

Goosebumps formed along Mina's forearms as her trembling fingers pulled her laptop close and pounded the keyboard.

"What are you doing?"

"Whatever I can to get back to Clover as soon as possible."

Just when an airline website popped up on the screen, Emma's eight-year-old daughter Giselle came bursting into the conference room.

"Mina! Mina!" she screamed. "We were just at The Icicle Café and saw all the stuff we're gonna use to make the gingerbread houses this weekend!"

Mina looked up from her computer and straightened her hunched shoulders. "You did? Tell me all about it!" she said before grabbing her phone.

"Hey, Karen, I'll call you back. Thanks for the intel."

"No problem. Let me know if you need help booking that flight home."

"Will do." Mina disconnected the call then turned her attention back to Giselle. "So what'd you see?"

"There were all these big bags of flour, and tubes of icing, and so much candy! I think I counted a hundred bags of gumdrops, peppermints, lollipops, jelly beans—"

"Giselle!" Emma interrupted after appearing in the doorway. "Why are you disturbing Mina while she's trying to work?"

"Because I wanted to tell her about all the gingerbread house ingredients we saw at the café."

"Yes, everything looked delicious. But we should let Mina get back to work."

"No, it's okay. I could actually use a break."

Emma entered the room and wrapped her arm around Giselle. "Mina, you should know that your workshop has this entire town in a complete uproar. In a good way, of course. The event sold out within thirty minutes of Scott posting it on the website. He had to add additional seating, but I still don't think there's going to be enough space."

"That's why he's gonna ask you to do *two* workshops," Giselle said while holding up two fingers.

"He sure is. I forgot about that. Mina, do you think you'd be up for holding two workshops?"

Mina studied the excited expressions on their faces. "I uh…I think so," she told them, unable to admit that she was planning on skipping town.

"Yay!" Giselle screamed while jumping up and down. "I'm going to both workshops."

Emma grabbed Giselle by the hand and led her toward the door. "Not unless everyone else who wants to participate gets to attend at least one. Now come on. Let's let Mina get back to work."

"Thanks ladies," Mina said just as her cell phone buzzed. It was a text from Scott.

Hey, great news! The gingerbread house workshop is so in demand that I had to add a second session. Think you can swing that? It'll mean two personal baking lessons as prizes from you as well, so I hope that's okay. Let me know. You're fast becoming the queen of Gosberg, Richards!

"Ugh," she groaned, laying her head down against the table. When her laptop pinged, she popped up and saw an email notification from Stephen appear on the screen. She opened it immediately.

Hello Mina,

Mitchell and I were wondering when you'll be back in town. We met with the execs from Henderson today, and they've decided to settle their case rather than go to trial. We all want to get this wrapped up ASAP. Let us know your plan. If you can't make it back soon, we'll have to pass this case on to another attorney. Thank you.

Mina's heart began to thump erratically. She took several deep breaths, then grabbed her phone and typed out a response to Scott.

I'm glad to hear everyone's so excited about the workshop. But unfortunately, I just received an email from the law firm, and I may have to fly back to Clover ASAP.

Mina sent the text, then typed an email message to Stephen.

> *Thank you for your message, sir. I am happy to hear that Henderson has decided to settle and feel confident that I can negotiate a very generous compensation package with the defendant. I'm looking to book a flight home now and will be arriving back in Clover soon. I'll keep you posted on the exact date. Thank you.*

As soon as she sent the email, Mina's phone buzzed again. It was a text from Scott.

That is such a bummer. Everyone's gonna be so disappointed when they find out you have to leave…

Before Mina could respond to the text, her computer pinged again. It was a response from Stephen.

> *I'd sent that email to you several hours ago. When I didn't hear back in a timely manner, we had no choice but to pass the Henderson case on to another lawyer. Jeff is now handling it.*

"*What*?" Mina yelled. She pounded her fist against the table then picked up the phone and called the front desk.

"Good evening, Emma's Bed and Breakfast, this is Charles speaking. How may I be of service?"

"Hey Charles, it's Mina," she panted, her high-pitch tone a clear indication that she was on the verge of losing it. "Was the internet down at all today?"

"You know, we actually did have an outage for a few hours. But we had our computer consultant come out and take a look at it, and we're back up and running now. Why? Is everything okay?"

Mina slumped down in her chair and stared up at the ceiling in disbelief. "No. Everything is not okay. But there's nothing I can do about it now."

"Aw, I'm so sorry to hear that. Well, let us know if there's anything we can do to help you out. In the meantime, Emma just cooked up a fresh pot of spicy chili. So if you're hungry and wanna take a break, feel free to come down and grab a bowl."

"Thanks, Charles."

Mina hung up the phone and balled her hands into tight fists, willing herself not to cry. She contemplated calling her parents but decided against it. They were under enough stress trying to manage her father's recovery. The last thing she wanted to do was dump more stress off on them.

Her cell phone buzzed again, and a text message from Scott appeared.

*Do you think I should cancel the workshops? *Sad face**

She sat still for several moments while contemplating his question, then typed a reply.

No, don't cancel just yet. I'm still trying to figure everything out on my end. I'll let you know soon.

And with that, she shut down her computer, gathered her things, and headed downstairs to try and sort everything out over a bowl of spicy chili.

Chapter Nine

MINA AND SCOTT walked slowly in between the tables that were tightly packed throughout The Icicle Café. It was Saturday afternoon, and the second set of workshop attendees were busy putting the final touches on their gingerbread houses.

"You guys are doing an amazing job," Mina told the group. "Scott and I are going to have a really hard time choosing a winner."

"Pick me! Pick me!" Lea yelled from the front of the café, which prompted several other contestants to follow suit.

"Okay guys, calm down," Scott said through an amused chuckle. "Now, in my book, you're all winners. But unfortunately, we can only choose one."

"Ugh," the crowd groaned in unison.

Mina leaned down and suggested to Mrs. Klein that she stick a few extra gumdrops onto her roof. Then she walked around to the other side of the table and asked Mary if she wanted to add white icing to the top of her chimney.

"Ooh, that's a great idea!" Mary told her. "That'll give it a nice snowy effect."

"Exactly," Mina agreed. When she moved on to the next attendee, she noticed Scott staring at her intently. Mina quickly looked away, pulling her hair behind her ear self-consciously.

After the pair finished making their rounds, they headed to the front of the café.

"All right, everyone," Mina said. "Scott and I are going to compare notes and add up the scores, and we'll be announcing the winner of the contest very soon. So stay tuned."

Scott followed her behind the bakery counter. "So what do you think? Whose gingerbread house do you like the best?"

"I love what Mrs. Weber and her daughter Sophia did. Their house looks like an elaborate yet cozy Christmas cottage. They get extra points in my book for adding their own miniature evergreens and faux snow. And the little Santa falling down the chimney head first with his legs hanging out of the top is so creative."

"Yes, that was genius. I actually chose them as my winners."

"Great minds think alike," Mina told him.

"Yes they do," Scott said, his gaze once again fixated on her.

She cleared her throat and looked back out at the attendees. "Would you like to do the honors of announcing the winner?"

"Sure." He gave her a wink, and together they walked back over to the front of the café. "Okay everyone, first of all, I'd like to thank you all for coming out and participating in today's workshop. This has by far been our best turnout yet. And now, without further ado, the first prize winner of the gingerbread house-building contest is...Mrs. Weber and her daughter Sophia!"

The mother and daughter duo squealed with delight while the rest of the participants gave them a standing ovation.

"Congratulations, you two!" Mina said. "I'm looking forward to our baking lesson tomorrow."

"So are we," Sophia said. "Thank you so much!"

As the crowd chatted and began packing up their gingerbread houses, Mina patted her damp forehead.

"Whew! I am exhausted," she sighed, "But I had such a good time. This was awesome."

"It really was. And you, my friend, were the belle of the ball. All of Gosberg has fallen in love with you. They're never gonna let you leave. You do know that, don't you?"

"That is really sweet of you to say. At the rate I'm going, that might not be a bad thing. Because since I've been in Gosberg, I have lost two of my cases to my biggest office rival. I'm honestly starting to feel as if that partnership is slowly slipping away."

Scott moved in closer to Mina and gently wrapped his arm around her. "I'm so sorry. I know how hard you've been working, and you didn't deserve that. But you know what I think?"

"What's that?" she asked, trying to ignore the tingling feeling that ran across her back underneath his touch.

"I think you should just enjoy this moment. Celebrate the incredible day you've had while doing something you truly love. Stop stressing about what's going on back in Clover."

"That's easier said than done considering my entire future is wrapped up in that partnership. But, I can try."

Scott gave her shoulder a squeeze. "And that's all you can do. Now, tell me. What are you doing tonight?"

"Working, I guess. Why?"

"Let me take you out. As a thank you. You have been so generous since you've been in town. All the baking, helping out with the customers, the workshops you conducted today. You've been outstanding."

"Don't forget about the baking lessons I'm conducting tomorrow for the gingerbread house contest winners," Mina added before playfully bumping Scott with her elbow. "But seriously, I could use a nice night out."

"Good. Why don't I swing by Emma's and pick you up at around seven?"

"Seven sounds good. Where are we going?"

"Stop being so nosy, Richards. It's a surprise. But for now, why don't we wrap things up around here and get you back to the bed and breakfast so you can get some work done?"

"Good idea," Mina said.

She spun on her heel and sauntered toward the back of the café, adding a little swing in her hips as Scott watched her walk away.

"MM, THAT WAS delicious," Mina told Scott as they exited Fisch's By The Sea restaurant. "I haven't had pickled herring since my parents and I left Gosberg."

"Glad you enjoyed it. I thought that partaking in a meal outside of The Icicle Café and Emma's would be a nice change of pace for you."

Mina slipped on her leather gloves. "Not that I don't love the food at both, but it definitely was. Thank you."

She looked up at the bright yellow streetlamps and watched as snowflakes slowly began to fall. "I don't think I'm ready for the night to end. What else do you think we should—"

Before she could finish the question, Mina heard the sound of hooves clicking against the asphalt. She spun around and laid eyes on a beautiful white horse-drawn carriage as it rounded the corner and stopped in front of the restaurant.

"Funny you should mention not wanting the night to end," Scott told her, "because neither do I." He held out his hand. "Madame, your chariot awaits."

Mina gasped with delight. She placed her hand in his and climbed inside the carriage. Scott cozied up next to her, then placed a wool blanket over their laps.

"Good evening," the driver said.

"Good evening," the pair replied. Scott gave him a thumbs up and the driver pulled the reins, guiding the horse away from the curb.

"You know," Scott said, "even though you hadn't planned on being in Gosberg this long, it's been really nice having you here."

"Thank you. It's been really nice being back. If it weren't for all the drama going on at the law firm, I'm sure I'd be having an even better time."

Scott slowly nodded his head. "I can certainly relate to that considering what's going on with the café. I still can't believe that there's a possibility it'll no longer be in existence."

Mina felt her body tense up. She didn't want to broach the subject of the café being sold.

"Hey, relax," Scott told her. "I'm not going to dwell on that. I just wanted to share with you how I was feeling. So, tell me, outside of the law firm, how's life in Clover, California?"

"Life in Clover is...interesting. Before arriving in Gosberg, I was in a great relationship with a man I thought I'd marry, expecting to be named partner, and my father hadn't fallen off of a ladder. But now—"

"Whoa, whoa, whoa, hold on a minute," Scott interrupted. "Did I just hear you say that you're in a great relationship with a man you expected to marry?"

"*Was* in a great relationship. We broke up right before I came to Gosberg."

"Really? Care to share what happened?"

Mina shifted in her seat. She hadn't really discussed the details of her breakup with anyone and wasn't prepared to talk about it now. "Honestly? Not really…"

"Hey, no pressure. I didn't mean to pry. I was just curious to know how someone could be crazy enough to let you go."

She glanced up at Scott as her lips curled into a soft smile. "That was nice of you to say. Thank you."

"Well, it's the truth." He reached over and brushed a snowflake from her eyelash. "I've known you for a long time. It's no secret that you're a great catch."

"Now you're just trying to butter me up so I'll spill all the juicy details."

He threw his hands in the air and chuckled lightly. "Fine. You caught me. I'm busted. But no, seriously, I completely understand if it's something you'd rather not discuss."

Mina's expression turned serious. She could see the sincerity and concern in Scott's eyes. It put her at ease, and she suddenly felt compelled to tell him what happened between her and Calvin.

"Long story short, my ex is also an attorney. He recently made partner at his firm, and instead of supporting my dream of making partner as well, he told me I should just quit altogether."

"Why would he do that?"

"Because he wanted me to start *focusing on our future*, which meant quitting work so that I could set up shop as a housewife. And not that there's anything wrong with being a housewife. But that's just never been my dream."

"Well that's understandable considering how ambitious and talented you are." Scott paused for a few moments before continuing. "Do you see yourself getting married and having children one day?"

"Oh, absolutely. It just has to be under the right circumstances, and with the right man, of course."

"Of course."

The twosome held each other's gaze until Mina felt the carriage make a sharp right turn. She looked up and saw that they were entering Union Street Park.

Blankets of sparkling white snow covered the benches and playground. Couples held hands as they skated around the rink. Mina was overcome by a warm, sweet sentiment as she took in the beauty of it all.

"So tell me," she said to Scott, "Why aren't you seeing anyone? Judging from the way all your Icicle Café patrons love cozying up to you, I'm surprised you're single."

"Cozying up to me? I don't know about all that. But I guess I've been so busy focusing on the café that I haven't even thought about dating."

"I'm sure all the women of Gosberg are thinking about it for you. How many times has someone tried to hook you up with a friend or relative over the years?"

"More than I can count," Scott said before he and Mina burst out laughing.

"I knew it. But I've noticed a certain someone who really seems to have her eye on you."

"Really. And who would that be?"

"Lillian."

"Lillian who?"

"Lillian the barista!"

When Scott stared at Mina cluelessly, she rolled her eyes. "Are you being serious right now? Lillian from the café!"

"Ohh, that Lillian! *Nooo*. She's not into me. She just loves working there and is very passionate about her job."

"Is that what you're gonna go with?"

"What do you mean?"

"Is that how you're gonna play it? Like you are completely oblivious to the fact that Lillian's got a huge crush on you?"

Scott shrugged his shoulders. "That's the only way I can play it, because I have no idea what you're talking about."

"Okay. Fine. I'll let it go and get back to you being single. Now that you won't have the burden of running the café, you'll have plenty of time to settle down and find yourself a girlfriend. Maybe you could try one of those dating apps or something."

"Um, no. That'll be a hard pass. I've heard so many horror stories from friends who've gone that route."

"Yeah, so have I. I've been so wrapped up in making partner that I haven't really dwelled on my breakup or worried about meeting someone new."

"I hear you. I've been so focused on trying to keep The Icicle Café in business that dating is the last thing on my mind."

"So tell me," Mina began, "*if* I stay in town long enough to attend The Icicle Fest, what sales pitch are we going to use in order to woo Felix into partnering with you?"

Scott wrapped his arm around Mina and pulled her in closer. "*When* you stay in town long enough to attend The Icicle Fest, we'll explain to Felix how The Icicle Café is so much more than just great food and fun novelty items. It is a second home to the residents of Gosberg. It's a gathering place that gives them a sense of community. A sense of family. And comfort..."

Mina slowly nodded her head. "That sounds perfect. Then once Felix and his family actually experience The Icicle Fest, it's game over. He'll be all in."

"That's the goal," Scott said as he gently caressed Mina's arm.

Even through her wool coat, she could feel the warmth

of his touch. She laid her head against his chest, and the pair took in the rest of the carriage ride in serene silence.

"Mr. Dawson, we've arrived at your first destination. Emma's Bed and Breakfast."

"Thank you."

Mina and Scott gradually pulled away from one another.

"Thank you again for tonight," she told him. "I had such a nice time."

"You're very welcome. And so did I."

The driver opened the carriage door and helped Mina out. Scott followed her, and together they walked up the stairs and entered the lobby.

"Will I see you tomorrow?" he asked.

"I'd like that. But I do need to start researching a new case, and I really have to give it my undivided attention. I can't lose this one like I did the other two."

"Understood," he said before leaning in and planting a soft kiss on her cheek. "Goodnight, Mina."

"Goodnight, Scott."

She spun around and floated up to her room, contemplating all the ways she could convince Felix to partner up with Scott during the festival.

Chapter Ten

MINA PROPPED HER pillows up against the bed's headboard and sat back. She dragged her computer onto her lap, logged onto Anderson & Moore's website and entered the passcode that opened her personal case file. The Sayer's Simulated Ski Slope document popped up. She double-clicked on it and scrolled down to the section titled Patent Infringement Accusations.

The minute she began reading, her cell phone buzzed. It was an incoming video chat from her parents. She grabbed the phone and accepted it.

"Hey guys!" Mina exclaimed. "I miss you all. What's going on?"

"Miss you too!" they said in unison.

Her mother blew kisses at the screen. "Sorry we didn't catch your call earlier. Your father and I were out meeting with our financial advisor."

"We're researching all the different ways we can invest the money we're going to collect after the sale of the café," her father said.

"I'm sure you two are having a ton of fun with that."

Mina slid her laptop off to the side of the bed. "Dad, how's your back?"

"Much better. I was actually able to drive for the first time today. So the meds and physical therapy are working."

Lynn reached over and patted Jake's back. "Not to mention all the massages your father has talked me into giving him day after day. Once he's fully recovered, he's gonna owe me. *Big* time."

"I've got you, babe," he said, kissing her forehead then turning back to the screen. "So what's going on with you, Mimi? How are things in Gosberg?"

"Things are good here. I've actually been spending a lot of time at the café. Believe it or not, I've even done some baking for the townspeople."

Lynn covered her mouth and acted as if she were about to fall off the couch. "Wait, you did *what*?"

"I baked a few of my specialties at the café!" Mina said, laughing as her father feigned a fainting spell.

"And what exactly did you make?" Lynn asked.

"Well, after realizing that your famous red velvet cupcakes are no longer on the menu, I baked several batches of those. And they were a huge hit."

"If you followed my recipe, I'm sure they were."

Jake abruptly sat up. "I'm reviving myself so that I can rejoin this conversation and find out what else you made," he said, glancing over at Lynn. "Can you believe what you're hearing right now?"

"No, I can't. Especially after we had to practically beg her to go to Gosberg in the first place."

"Hey, I can still hear you two."

"Sorry, sweetheart," Lynn said. "We're just in a bit of shock. So go on. Tell us more."

"I also whipped up a few batches of my blizzard brownies. And you'll *really* be surprised to hear that I built the most amazing gingerbread house, which I used as an example during a how-to workshop that I conducted. At the end of the tutorial, Scott and I held a contest, and I gifted the winners with baking lessons."

Lynn reached over and gripped Jake's arm. "I'm totally speechless. I cannot believe this. Our girl is back in Gosberg, baking desserts and conducting workshops at The Icicle Café. I love it!"

"I can't believe it either," Jake said. "We're glad you finally had a chance to spend some time there before the café closes its doors."

"Me, too," Mina said. "It's actually been fun hanging out with Scott, too."

"Ooh, *Scott*," Lynn gushed, nudging Jake mischievously. "I can only imagine how much you've enjoyed getting reacquainted with him."

Mina pointed at the screen. "Mom, please don't start with that."

"Yes, honey, give her a break," Jake added.

"Thanks, dad," Mina said with a giggle, watching as her

parents nudged one another playfully. "Listen, I'd better get going. I've got a lot of work to do."

"Speaking of work, how are things going with the firm?" Lynn asked. "Any news on when your partnership is going to be announced?"

"Things actually aren't that great. Since I've been in Gosberg, two of my cases were handed off to another attorney. So if I even want to be in the running to make partner at this point, I need to get back to Clover and knock my current case out the park."

"And I take full responsibility for you having to stay in Gosberg longer than expected after I mixed up the dates of The Icicle Fest," Lynn admitted. "I still cannot believe I did that. What was I thinking?"

"You were thinking about my back," Jake told her. "But listen, Mimi, if anybody can do it, you can. Just stay focused and keep giving your cases your all. You deserve that partnership, and we have no doubt that you're going to get it."

"Thank you. I'll keep grinding, knowing that everything is going to work in my favor."

"That's our girl," Lynn said. "Love you, baby. Talk soon."

"Love you, too."

Mina blew her parents a kiss and disconnected the video chat. Just when she contemplated calling Scott, her laptop pinged and an email from Karen popped up on the screen. The message was sent high priority. Mina's stomach dropped down to her knees. She held her breath and opened the message.

Hey! Just checking in to see how things are going with the Sayer's Ski Slope case. The partners have asked me to attend a last-minute meeting in your place, and a few select attorneys are going to be there, Jeff included. I'd love to give them an update if you've got one. Let me know ASAP! Hope all is going well and you'll be home soon. XO

Mina quickly clicked on the Sayer case file and opened every document inside of it.

"This is your chance, girl," she told herself. "Time to kick it into high gear."

She sent Karen a message letting her know she'd be emailing an update within thirty minutes.

Perfect, Karen wrote back. *And I know you're a pro, but don't forget to focus on how you're going to attack the defendant's patent infringement on Sayer's at-home online classes, the ski machine's screen style, and the exercise program options.*

"See, this is why I love you," Mina said to herself before responding to the message.

Already on it. Thank you for always having my back. I'll be in touch soon. XO

She sent the message, then got to work on her report.

MINA CLOSED HER laptop and fell back onto the bed. She was exhausted. She'd spent several hours composing Sayer's patent litigation strategy, and emailed it along with a video conference invitation to the partners requesting they review it together. Mina cc'd Karen on the message, who responded with a slew of accolades.

This is it! her email read. *You NAILED your plan of attack. I love it. I'll do everything I can to make sure we get that video conference scheduled immediately. Chat soon!*

The minute Mina felt herself drifting off to sleep, her cell phone buzzed. She grabbed it and opened one eye. A text message from Scott appeared on the screen.

Good evening! Have you eaten dinner yet? If not, feel free to stop by the café. We're serving chicken breast Schnitzel and it's going fast. If you can make it, I'll set a plate aside for you. Let me know…

Mina was tired, but she was also hungry. And The Icicle Café's chicken breast Schnitzel was one of her favorite dishes.

After thinking it over for several minutes, she decided to go to the café. It would be nice to get out of her room, mingle with the townspeople and enjoy a good meal.

But as she climbed out of bed, Mina realized that more than anything, she was most looking forward to hanging out with Scott.

Chapter Eleven

"HEY!" SCOTT SAID to Mina when she approached him in the middle of Union Street Park. "You look great. Do I spy a new coat, *and* a new pair of boots?"

Mina ran her hands down the sleeves of her puffy red bomber jacket and kicked up her feet, showing off her black leather snow boots. "Why yes, you do. I didn't expect to be in Gosberg this long, and I finally came to the conclusion that I hadn't packed enough warm clothes. So I went to Martha's Wintery Flair this morning and, as you can see, she hooked me up."

Scott eyed Mina from head to toe, his lips spreading into a sexy smile. "Yes she did. I like it."

His gaze brought on a sudden bout of shyness as Mina fiddled with the zipper on her coat and glanced down at his feet. "Thanks. So uh, I see you brought out the old wooden sled from back in the day. I can't believe you held on to it after all these years."

"Of course I did. Why would I ever let go of Flash Lightning? We've had some great times together, flying up and down these hills."

"You and Flash Lightning?"

"Yes, me and Flash Lightning." Scott paused, eyeing Mina suspiciously. "Wait, are you making fun of me, Richards?"

"Now why would I do that?" she quipped, swatting his shoulder playfully. "Anyway, how are we going to tackle this sledding mission? Are we gonna start off small then go big like we used to do as kids? Or are we going to risk it all and tackle Union Street's steepest hill first?"

"Go big or go home, baby. Right?"

"I guess..." Mina glanced up at the hill. "Just keep in mind I haven't done this in a long time, so don't topple this thing over and injure me. I'd like to return to Clover in one piece."

"I got you. Come on. Let's do it." Scott offered Mina his arm, and together they headed up the hill.

"I haven't been sledding in years," he said. "But I figured since you've been under so much pressure with work and I've been so wrapped up in the café, we both needed this. Wouldn't you agree?"

"Absolutely."

When they reached the top of the hill, Scott dropped the sled down onto the snow. "Have a seat, Richards. I'm about to take you on the ride of your life."

"Ha! Is that what you're about to do?"

"Yeah. It is. So hop on. Let me show you a good time."

"Okay. Let's ride."

Mina climbed inside the sled. Scott gave it a push before hopping in behind her. As they slid down the hill, she squealed with delight. And when Scott wrapped his arms around her tightly, Mina fell back against him, pushing all thoughts of work and the possible sale of the café out of her mind.

"THANKS SO MUCH," Scott said to the server at the park's snack shack. He handed Mina a cup of hot chocolate. "Now *that* was fun. I always knew I was a sledding champion, but I had no clue I was still so good at it."

"Okay, I'll let you have that. You definitely held it down as the captain of the sled. So, cheers to you." Mina held her cup in the air and tapped it against his. "And by the way, you were right. I did need this today. It's been nice not having to think about what's happening back at the law firm."

"You have no idea how happy I am to hear that."

Scott placed his hand on the small of her back and led Mina toward the playground area. She relished in the sound of children's laughter, watching as they flew through the air on swing sets and bounced up and down on seesaws. But the pleasant moment came to an abrupt end when Mina pulled her cell phone from her pocket and checked the time.

"Oh no," she moaned. "I didn't realize how late it had

gotten. I need to get back to Emma's. I've got a video conference scheduled with the partners to discuss the case I'm working on."

Scott's hand slowly slid off her back and down by his side. "Oh, okay."

She could hear the disappointment in his voice. Mina reached out and gave his arm a squeeze. "I'll tell you what. Why don't I come by the café tonight for dinner?"

"I'll do you one better. Why don't you come over to my place for dinner tonight? I'll prepare something special for you. Plus it'll be nice and quiet, so we'll have some privacy."

"I'd like that," Mina said, flattered by the invitation.

"Awesome. Now all I have to do is come up with something spectacular to prepare."

"Please don't go out of your way to make anything fancy. We can keep it simple."

Scott flashed Mina a cocky smirk. "I don't even know what simple means when it comes to my cooking."

"Okay then, master chef! Well if you're going to go all out, how about I make something too? Maybe I can whip up a batch of my sparkling white chocolate lemon truffles for dessert."

"Wait," Scott said, squinting his eyes suspiciously, "While those do sound delicious, I think you might be trying to outdo me. Is that what's happening here, Richards?"

"No! Not at all." She laughed. "But look, I need to get going. I cannot be late for this video conference. It's make-

or-break time for me at the firm."

"Can I give you a ride?"

"Emma let me borrow her car, so I'm good. But thanks. What time should I be at your place tonight?"

"How does seven o'clock sound?"

"Seven o'clock sounds perfect. But what about the café? However will they survive without you?" she joked.

"Listen, Mary is like my copilot. I think she runs the café smoother than I do. So don't worry. They'll be fine. Which is a good thing. Because all I want to focus on is my evening with you."

Mina felt her knees give a bit underneath the weight of Scott's words. "Same here," she replied softly. "Thanks again for this afternoon, and I'll see you tonight."

"I'm looking forward to it."

He leaned in and gave her a lingering hug. Just when he went to kiss her cheek, she turned her head, and his lips caught the corner of her mouth. She quickly pulled away and pressed her hands against his chest.

"Ooh," she uttered. "I'm so sorry. I uh…have a uh…have a great rest of the day."

"Thank you." He snickered. "You have a great rest of the day as well. Good luck with your video conference."

"Thanks."

Mina spun around and struggled to stroll gracefully through the heavy snow. When she reached the car, she looked over her shoulder and saw that Scott was watching her. He raised his hand and waved goodbye. She waved back, then climbed inside the car and pulled off.

On the way back to Emma's, Mina shifted her focus and began running strategies through her mind that she planned on presenting to the partners. But no matter how hard she tried, her brain just kept drifting back to thoughts of Scott.

MINA POSITIONED HER laptop perfectly on top of the desk. She took a quick look in the mirror and made sure every hair was in place, her makeup was properly set, and her blazer was pressed to perfection.

Good to go...

She sat down and logged into the video conferencing system, then typed in her password. A few seconds later, the Anderson & Moore conference room popped up on the screen. Stephen and Mitchell were sitting next to one another at the head of the table. Karen was sitting to their right, and each of their assistants were sitting off to the side of her. And then, much to Mina's surprise, Jeff was sitting to their left.

She balled her hands into tight fists and exhaled slowly. *Stay calm. Be cool. Stay calm. Be cool,* she thought to herself over and over again.

"Mina!" Stephen boomed. "It's so wonderful to see you. Your presence is sorely missed around here."

"Indeed it is," Mitchell chimed in. "As a matter of fact, we thought you would've been back by now."

Mina ran her damp palms over her skirt and forced a pleasant smile. "Hello, everyone. I certainly miss being there. I thought I'd be back in Clover by now as well. But as soon as I get things squared away with our family's business, I'll be back."

"We should hope so," Mitchell said, tapping his pen against the table. "Because for a minute there, I was beginning to wonder whether you'd jumped ship and decided to move back to Germany!"

"Why would she do that?" Stephen asked him before turning his attention back to Mina. "Isn't it snowy and freezing cold there?"

"It is," she replied. "But no worries. Moving to Gosberg is not in the cards for me. I'll be back in California just as soon as I can."

"Well lucky for you, Mina," Jeff chimed in, "I've been holding down the fort just fine in your absence. I was able to win both the Perfect Pitch and Henderson cases." He shrugged his shoulders and looked over at Stephen and Mitchell. "*And* I was able to pull all that off at the last minute, with no time to do the proper research!"

Mina dug her fingernails into her thighs as she glared at Jeff's chubby bearded face. She glanced over at Karen, who looked as if she wanted to jump across the table and strangle him.

"And we appreciate how you've stepped up to help out the firm, Jeff," Stephen told him. "Now Mina, back to you. We've all had a chance to take a look at your Sayer's Ski Slope write-up, and we love your plan of attack. It's clear to us that you really analyzed the company's products. The strategic way in which you broke down each of the defendant's patent infringements was genius."

Mina sat up straighter and folded her hands on top of the desk. "Thank you, Stephen. I appreciate that."

"I've got a question for you," Mitchell said. "I noticed that in your write-up, you focused solely on the patent infringements that Sayer filed against the defendant. After studying both companies so closely, were you able to discover any other possible breaches committed by the defendant that Sayer may have overlooked?"

Mina sat back in her chair, contemplating the odd question. As a patent litigation attorney, it wasn't her job to search for infringements against companies. She was responsible for representing companies in court who'd already established the fact that their product had been infringed upon.

She grabbed her tablet and double-clicked on the Sayer case file. "My main focus has been on the violations that Sayer actually filed against the defendant. Those include the online classes, the style of the machine's screen display and its exercise program options."

"If I may please chime in for a moment here," Jeff interjected.

Mina zoomed in on Mitchell and noticed him giving Jeff a discreet head nod.

What was that? she almost blurted out before biting her jaw and remaining silent.

"Sure Jeff, go ahead," Mitchell said.

"Thank you. So, as I was researching the Sayer file…"

Why are you researching yet another one of my cases? Mina was dying to yell at the screen.

"…I noticed that the defendant's ski machine utilizes a leaderboard display for users that is very similar to the one that Sayer created."

"And what exactly is a leaderboard display?" Stephen asked Jeff.

"It's an interactive digital screen that's attached to the ski machines. The purpose is to allow users to keep up with one another's workout progress. The companies also use it to keep clients motivated during their workouts."

"Hm, interesting," Mitchell said. "Mina? Do you know anything about this?"

Mina's entire body was overcome by a hot wave of panic. She focused in on Jeff, who was staring back at her with the smuggest sneer she'd ever seen.

She snatched up her tablet and began sliding through the Sayer documents, knowing full well she had no information on leaderboard displays, in an attempt to buy some time. "Let me uh…let me see what notes I took on that…"

"Actually," Karen said, vigorously tapping away at the keys on her laptop, "Mina and I discussed both companies' leaderboard displays a few days ago. I took the notes on that, so I can pull them up really quickly now."

Mina stared at Karen in awe. They had not discussed a thing about leaderboards. But considering Karen was the best, most thorough assistant at the firm, Mina wasn't a bit surprised that she'd researched every single aspect of the ski machines.

"We did a data analysis of Sayer's leaderboard display versus the defendant's," Karen continued. "First off, the defendant's leaderboard was invented before Sayer's, and they haven't performed any updates since its inception."

"Really?" Mitchell uttered, peeking over at Jeff curiously.

"Secondly," she continued, "The defendant's board focuses primarily on users' fat burning percentages, ski speed and style. Sayer's board focuses on calories burned, proper form and level of difficulty."

Karen discreetly turned toward the screen and gave Mina a slight wink. Mina caught the hint and picked up where Karen left off.

"So after that extensive assessment, Karen and I didn't discover any similarities between the two companies' leaderboard displays."

Mina curled her toes excitedly inside her slippers, resisting the urge to kiss Karen through the computer screen.

Stephen pointed at Jeff, and all eyes in the room turned

to him. "So what is it about the defendant's leaderboard display that you think they ripped off from Sayer, Jeff?"

Mina leaned in closer to the computer. She could see droplets of sweat forming along Jeff's thinning hairline. His chest was heaving in and out as if he were hyperventilating. He stared blankly at Stephen for several seconds before finally speaking up.

"Well I uh, I just ascertained that the defendant's leaderboard was proving to display live ski events and users' workout progress in a way that's eerily similar to Sayer's."

"Do you have the data analytics to back up your claim?" Stephen pressed.

Jeff looked to Mitchell, who was busy staring down at his cell phone.

"Um, I uh…I think my assistant may have been working on that for me. Let me check with her."

"You do that," Stephen said, his wavering tone filled with doubt. "But in the meantime, Mina, you did a phenomenal job on this write-up. We're going to pass it along to Sayer for their approval. Can you make yourself available if they have questions for you?"

"Absolutely, sir."

"Good. And when do you think you'll be back in Clover? You worked really hard on this case, and I'd love to see you represent them in court."

"I'll get back to you with a definite date just as soon as I have one."

"Be sure to keep us posted on that."

"Will do."

"Great work, Mina," Mitchell said. "Looking forward to you bringing this one home for the team."

Her eyebrows shot up in surprise. The last thing she'd expected was a compliment from Jeff's biggest cheerleader.

"Thank you, Mitch. I really appreciate you and everyone else getting together with me in order to review this case. I'll be in touch soon."

The minute Mina ended the video conference, she hopped out of her chair and jumped around the room in celebration of her win. Once she got it all out, she sent Karen a text message thanking her profusely for saving the day. Karen wrote back within seconds.

You're welcome, sis! I was just being a queen, straightening my fellow queen's crown. Now hurry back so you can lock down this partnership!

Mina's fingers flew over the keys as she shimmied with excitement.

I will! As soon as I figure out exactly when I'll be back, you'll be the first to know.

Mina sent the message then glanced over at the clock, noticing it was time to start getting dressed.

A slight thrill shot through her at the thought of having dinner at Scott's. And that's when Mina realized whatever she was feeling for him had moved well beyond the friend zone.

Chapter Twelve

THESE STILETTO PUMPS were not a good idea, Mina thought to herself while climbing the stairs to Scott's house. Thankfully he'd shoveled the snow surrounding his property. Nevertheless, the slippery ground was still difficult to maneuver.

"That's what I get for trying to be cute," she muttered after ringing the bell. Within seconds, he opened the door.

"Hey you," he said, holding out his hand and helping her inside. "Thanks again for coming. You look beautiful."

"Thank you," Mina replied, trying not to swoon after inhaling his woodsy cologne. She looked around Scott's beautifully decorated, rustic townhouse. "Your home is lovely."

"Thanks, but I can't take much credit. I tossed out a few ideas to a very talented interior designer, and she brought them all to life. May I take your coat?"

"Yes, please."

As Scott helped Mina out of her coat, she could feel him eyeing her slim figure, which was clad in a fitted sleeveless magenta dress.

"Wow," he breathed. "You look beautiful."

She clasped her hands tightly in front of her and tried not to stare back at him. But she couldn't help but notice how handsome Scott looked with his freshly cut hair and trimmed goatee. He was dressed in a pale blue button-down shirt and perfectly tailored navy pants, both accentuating his athletic build.

"Thanks. You look really nice, too."

"Yeah, well, I thought you should know that I do own more than just the jeans and athletic wear you're used to seeing me in. Can I take that bag from you?"

"Sure. I stopped by the grocery store and picked up the ingredients for my white chocolate lemon truffles."

"You have no idea how much I'm looking forward to those." He grabbed the bag then took her hand in his. "Come on. I'll show you to the kitchen."

"Dinner smells delicious," she said. "What's on the menu?"

"Well I figured you'd probably had enough of The Icicle Café's German specialties. So I decided to switch it up tonight. We're having beef wellington wrapped in a crêpe, warm wilted winter greens, roasted potatoes with garlic and herbs, and a full-bodied dry red wine."

Mina's mouth began to water at the sound of it all. "That sounds sensational. Scott, you are amazing. Why aren't you working as an executive chef at a high-end restaurant in Paris or New York? You could be doing so much more than just managing our parents' little café."

He dropped the bag of groceries down on the counter. "Our parents' *little café*? Is that what you think of it? Mina, The Icicle Café is where it all started for me. That place enabled me to realize my dream of becoming a chef. And while I do have a classical culinary education, the café is where I truly honed my skills."

Mina's expression grew solemn as she reached inside the bag and pulled out her ingredients. "I'm sorry, Scott. I didn't mean to offend you. And I certainly didn't mean to talk down about our parents' café, or your efforts. It's just that—"

"You didn't offend me," he interrupted. "I heard the compliment within your statement, and I appreciate it. I also get that someone like you, who lives this big life in California and has cultivated a career in law, would think that working in some fancy restaurant is more meaningful than running *our parents' little café*. But since you've been away from Gosberg for so long, I don't think you truly understand the significance and value of the café. At least not anymore."

Mina slammed a bag of flour down onto the counter. "That could not be further from the truth, Scott. Just because my dreams kept me away from Gosberg doesn't mean I don't recognize the café's worth. So please don't make me out to be some uppity, out-of-touch snob because I'm motivating you to think bigger and chose to pursue a career in law."

"Speaking of which, how's that working out for you? Did

they name you partner during your video conference today?"

Mina froze. She glared at Scott, whose steely eyes were staring right back at her. Several moments passed, and they both remained silent. When Scott opened the bottle of wine, poured himself a glass and took a long gulp, she spun around and stormed into the living room.

"You know what?" she exclaimed, "I didn't come here for this." She snatched her coat off the rack and threw open the door. Right before she walked out, Scott grabbed her hand.

"Mina, please, don't leave. I'm sorry. I don't know what got into me. I mean, I do know, but…I shouldn't have taken it out on you. And I can explain myself."

She took a deep breath, contemplating whether she should stay. But before she'd made a decision, Scott gently took her coat and hung it back up.

Mina closed the door and let him lead her back into the kitchen.

"Dinner will be ready soon," he said. "In the meantime, why don't we enjoy a glass of wine?"

"Okay," she replied quietly, placing her hand over her chest in an effort to slow her heart rate. "I'll start preparing the truffles and get them refrigerated before we sit down to eat."

Mina was anxious to ask Scott what had prompted his outburst. But when she noticed his hands trembling as he poured her wine, she decided to wait and let him tell her in his own time.

He walked around the counter and handed her a glass. "So, do you accept my apology?"

"I do."

"Good. I hope I didn't put a damper on the night, because I've been looking forward to this all day."

"No, you didn't. And I've been looking forward to it, too."

The tension that Mina felt throughout her body gradually began to subside. She held her glass in the air and clinked it against Scott's.

"Cheers. Thanks again for having me over."

"Cheers to you. Thanks for coming. And staying."

Mina took a sip of wine and nodded her head. "Mm, this is really good. It's very hearty."

"I figured it would go well with the beef wellington."

"You made a great choice." She look another sip then set the glass down. "I'd better start whipping up my ingredients for the truffles."

"Cool. While you do that, I'll set the table and start putting out the food. It should be ready. Oh, by the way, I really want to hear how your video conference went."

"That sounds good. And I'll catch you up on the video conference during dinner. In the meantime, do you have a mixing bowl?"

"I do." Scott reached inside a cabinet, pulled down a stainless steel bowl and handed it to her. "Anything else you need to make these truffles that I'm going to completely devour?"

"Yes. A saucepan, a measuring cup and a large spoon. And as for the truffles, could you at least save me a few?"

"I'll try." Scott grabbed the rest of the things Mina requested and set them on the counter. When Mina brushed up against him while reaching for the measuring cup, he leaned in and planted a soft kiss on her cheek.

The unexpected gesture caused her to gasp ever so slightly. Her skin tingled underneath the feel of his lips.

"What was that for?" she asked softly.

"I forgot to do it when you walked through the door."

"Oh...okay."

A rush of heat crept up the back of Mina's neck. She struggled to maintain her composure while pouring flour inside the measuring cup.

"This is gonna be a long night," she muttered to herself, unable to take her eyes off of Scott as he swaggered into the dining room carrying a stack of plates.

MINA POPPED A truffle inside her mouth. "I think I may have gained a good five pounds tonight."

"I doubt that. You burned a ton of calories this afternoon while we were sledding. So no worries. You're good."

"Speaking of good, this *dinner* was good. No, actually, it

was amazing. Have you ever served beef wellington at the café?"

"No, I haven't. But come to think of it, this dish would be a great holiday menu option. Well it *would* have been. Unless Felix decides to partner with me, of course." Scott tilted his head to the side and gave Mina a sly smile. "So have you decided if you're going to stick around for The Icicle Fest and help me nail this deal?"

She watched him while twirling her glass around in her hand. "Still working on it. Everybody at the firm is riding me to get back to Clover as soon as possible. But things are going really well with my current case. So we'll see. I just may be able to pull it off."

Scott stood up and began clearing the dishes. "I'm keeping my eyes, fingers and toes crossed that you'll be able to make it happen."

"I'm gonna do my best," Mina said, grabbing their wine glasses and following him into the kitchen. "So tell me more about what goes on at The Icicle Fest. Exactly how is it going to entice Felix into doing business with you?"

"Let's see. Where do I even start? Well, there's an awesome parade with great floats that the community builds themselves, fun wintery games and fantastic prizes, vendor booths filled with unique crafts and edibles that are made by the townspeople, a ton of delicious food, a really cool DJ, and of course gourmet eats prepared by *moi*."

"That sounds very enticing. Felix and his family are going to be blown away after experiencing all of that." Mina paused for a moment and peered over at Scott. "Now that I've heard those tantalizing details, I think I can RSVP with a tentative yes."

"*Really?*" Scott yelled, grabbing Mina and hugging her tightly. "Yes! I knew I could somehow talk you into staying. Thank you, thank you, thank you!"

"It's not definite yet," Mina said, laughing into his shoulder, "but hopefully I can work something out."

"I know, I know. I just appreciate the effort."

Scott slowly pulled away from Mina but kept his arms wrapped around her waist. They stared at one another for several seconds until his cell phone buzzed.

"I'd better check that. It may be someone from the café."

"Okay," Mina said before heading into the dining room. As she cleared the table, she noticed that the muscles in her calves were trembling with excitement.

Girl, don't start, she told herself on the way back into the kitchen.

"Everything all right?" she asked Scott.

"Yep, everything's fine. That was Mary texting to let me know we had a packed house tonight."

"No surprise there."

"So listen," Scott said. "I've got a request."

"Oh do you now. What is it?"

"If you *are* able to attend The Icicle Fest, may I ask that you please treat the guests to some of your scrumptious white chocolate lemon truffles?"

"See, now you're trying to be slick and tie me down with obligations," Mina replied before they both burst out laughing. "But if I'm still in town, then yes, I'd be happy to. Actually, I'll do you one better. If I'm able to stay for the festival, I will help out with the planning as well. How does that sound?"

"Now *that* sounds incredible. We could definitely use your talents, and there's a lot that still needs to get done. Mary is going to be ecstatic when she finds out you're pitching in. If you're able to stay, that is."

"I will certainly try my best," Mina told him as she placed a plate inside the dishwasher then looked around the kitchen. "Looks like we're done here. Thank you again for dinner. I really enjoyed it."

"You're welcome. But wait, you're not getting ready to leave, are you?"

"I do need to get going. Karen and I have an early call in the morning. She's working with me on the Sayer case, and she may have some insight into whether I can swing being away for another week."

Scott closed his eyes and pressed his hands together. "Come on, Karen. Come through for a brother!"

Mina laughed as she and Scott headed into the living room. He helped her into her coat then walked her out to the car.

"You know," he said, "I really hope Karen can convince

you to stay. Because aside from the festival, I'm really not ready for you to leave yet. Oh, and as for that...*spirited* conversation we had earlier about the whole executive chef thing—"

"Scott, really I didn't mean to—"

"No, no, we don't have to rehash it. I know you didn't mean any harm. I just wanted to share something with you. Before I found out that our parents were selling The Icicle Café, I was planning to talk to them about partnering up to open a spinoff restaurant called The Icicle House. It was going to be an upscale eatery. The type of place where beef wellington is an everyday option on the menu."

"I love that idea. Hey, maybe you can still do it. You know, start your own thing from scratch."

"I could. But starting over would be really difficult. And costly. Especially if I'm going at it alone."

"That's okay. I think you should go for it anyway. You've already made a great name for yourself here in Gosberg. How hard could it be?"

"You'd be surprised at just how hard it is. But I've actually been seriously considering going into business for myself, just in case things don't work out with Felix. I've even thought about opening a pop-up restaurant or starting a catering business while I work on securing a loan and finding the perfect location for an upscale eatery."

"Well, you're one of the most intelligent and determined people I know, Scott. If you want it, you can have it. When it's all said and done, you're going to land on your feet and come out on top. Period."

"Thanks, Mina," he said. "I really appreciate your faith in me. It means a lot."

"I wish I could do more to help."

"You've already done more than enough just by being here and blessing us with your immense talents. Not to mention the fact that you're planning to stick around for the festival."

"It's been my pleasure. I certainly didn't expect to be in town this long, but I have to admit, I've had a great time. My mother said this trip was exactly what I needed to clear my head after all the drama I've been going through back home. I think she was right."

"I think she was, too. You know, it's funny, I was rather skeptical when you first came to town. I didn't know whether you'd be an ally or an enemy in my plight to keep the café. But now that it's coming down to the wire, I don't think I would've been able to get through all this without you."

"Aww, aside from the skeptical part, that was really sweet. Who knows, if things don't work out with Felix, maybe you'll consider moving back to the states and opening a restaurant there. You know that's your mother's number one goal, right?"

Scott rolled his eyes and chuckled softly. "Yes, I do. Trust me, she's made that very clear. But I honestly don't ever see myself leaving Gosberg. It's home for me. I'm really committed to this town and community."

"I really admire that about you. One way or another, I'm sure everything is going to work out just fine," Mina told him.

"You know, I think you're right…"

Light, fluffy snowflakes began to fall as Scott opened the car door. He kissed Mina gently on the cheek, and she climbed inside.

"Shoot me a text when you get to Emma's so that I'll know you made it there safely."

"I will. Thank you again for dinner. It was delicious."

"You're very welcome. Thank you for the dessert. It was delectable. Those truffles are gonna be a huge hit at the festival."

"I love your confidence. But as our moms always told us when we were kids—"

"*We'll see,*" Mina and Scott said in unison.

"Exactly!" Mina exclaimed. "All right, it's been real, but I've gotta go get some sleep. See you tomorrow?"

"See you tomorrow."

Mina waved at Scott and pulled away from the curb. She drove gingerly through the snow, brainstorming all the different ways she could convince the partners at the firm that she needed to stay in Gosberg one more week.

Chapter Thirteen

MINA SAT IN the middle of The Icicle Café's gift shop, slicing open a cardboard box while Mary looked on excitedly.

"I love it when we receive new merchandise!" Mary exclaimed, frantically clapping her hands. "And I personally chose all of these items myself, so I'm hoping they'll sell well."

"I'm sure they will, because you've got great taste," Mina told her. She reached inside the box and pulled out a crystal snowflake. "Ooh, this is beautiful. Is it a paperweight?"

Mary bent down so quickly that she almost tumbled over. "It can be used as a paperweight, decoration, ornament…it's a multipurpose piece. And it's *gooorgeous*. The photo on the Winter Enchantment's website did not do that snowflake justice. At all."

Mina unwrapped another crystal paperweight, which was in the shape of a snowman. "I love this, Mary! These fit the theme of the café perfectly."

"They do, don't they? We're putting them in the store for now, and whatever we have left over will be sold at The

Icicle Fest. If they sell out beforehand, then I'll just place another order for the festival."

"I definitely think these are going to sell out before the fest," Mina said after tearing the bubble wrap off of a crystal gingerbread man. "I want one of everything!"

"Wait until you see the glass mugs, keychains and pictures frames I ordered. I just might have to use my employee discount and buy one of everything, too!"

Mina stood up and began placing the new items on the shelves. "I didn't see the flyers and posters for the festival in any of the boxes. Have they already been delivered?"

"Yep, they're here. I opened that box before you came in and tasked Lillian with hanging the posters and passing out flyers to the customers."

"Oh, really? I asked her about them earlier, but she said she hadn't seen them."

Mary rolled her eyes. "That girl…" she mumbled while slicing open a box. "Ahh, the keychains!" She held a glass icicle in the air and dangled it back and forth. "Isn't this fantastic? I couldn't believe I found them!"

"*Yesss*! Those should be a permanent fixture here in the gift shop. You may as well put in another order now, because they're definitely going to sell out."

As soon as the words were out of her mouth Mina tightened her lips, reminding herself that she had to stop speaking on the café as if it wasn't possibly closing.

"You're right. I'll do that now." Mary pull her cell phone

out of her back pocket and began typing away.

"Hey," Mina said, "I saw that little look you gave me when I brought up Lillian. What was that about?"

Mary huffed loudly. "I'm tired of that girl acting out toward you because of her little crush on Scott. Maybe she's heard all the rumblings around town about how you and Scott should be dating..."

Mina's eyebrows furrowed in confusion as she placed miniature snow globes on the shelf. "Oh, is that what the people are saying?"

"Maybe," she snorted before letting out a loud cackle. "But seriously, we all love you, Mina. And if you ask me, Scott does, too."

"I don't know about all that. But we've definitely enjoyed reconnecting with one another since I've been in town. But we live such different lives now. And I'll be going back to California soon."

"You'll still be in town for The Icicle Fest though, won't you?"

"Hopefully. I talked to my assistant at the firm earlier today, and it sounds like everything is in order with my current client. If that's the case, then yes, I'll be able to stay."

"Yay! And Scott bragged about those white chocolate lemon truffles you made all morning. He said you're going to make a big batch for the festival. If you're open to it, maybe we could sell them here one night this week as a little teaser. Wouldn't that be fun?"

"That would be fun," Mina said, tickled by Mary's enthusiasm.

"Hey, ladies," Scott said as he entered the gift shop carrying two mugs. "You all have been back here working so hard that I figured you could use a break."

"Perfect timing," Mary said. "Is that peppermint hot chocolate I smell?"

"It sure is." Scott handed her a mug, then Mina, who immediately took a sip of the sweet minty drink.

"Mm, this is really good," she said.

"Isn't it?" Scott agreed. "I'm embarrassed to admit that I just knocked back two cups while I was up front greeting guests. Lillian makes the best beverages I've ever tasted."

Mina was surprised by the twinge of jealousy she felt swirl inside her chest. She stirred her hot chocolate with a candy cane while watching Scott closely. As she eyed him, Mary eyed her with a knowing grin.

Stop that, Mina mouthed to her.

"So how's it going back here?" Scott asked. "Are we liking the new merchandise we ordered for The Icicle Fest kickoff week?"

"We're loving it," Mary gushed, pointing at the shelves. "Look at those stunning paperweights, mugs, and snow globes. Aren't they cool?"

"They are." He walked over to get a closer look. "Very cool. Everybody's gonna love them."

Mina took a few more sips of cocoa and set the cup

down on the counter. "Check out these keychains. The icicle charm is my favorite."

"Mine, too," Mary chimed in. "Mina actually suggested that we start carrying them in the gift shop year-round. I totally agree with her."

"Hm," Scott murmured quietly. "I'll uh…I'll think about it." He looked over at Mina, who stared back at him through wide eyes, indicating she'd slipped up.

"Hey, Mary," he continued a bit more cheerily, "You know those fun miniature Icicle Fest promotional signs you ordered?"

"The ones I'm going to display on top of the desserts? Yep. What about them?"

"They were just delivered. Lillian has already started placing them on the cupcakes and brownies, and they look really great."

"Ahh, *finally*!" she shrieked. "I have to go check them out. Mina, are you okay finishing up back here?"

"Of course. I'll just make Scott help me," she said, pinching his arm.

"Great. Thanks!"

Mina giggled while watching Mary scurry to the front of the café. "Is she always this ecstatic over The Icicle Fest?"

"Always," Scott confirmed. "Every year she tells me that she enjoys the festival more than Christmas day."

"Oh my. Now that is quite the compliment. I can't wait to experience it for myself."

"Wait, so does that mean you're staying for the fest?"

"Well, after my call with Karen this morning, it sounds like everything is in order regarding my client's case. They confirmed that they're willing to settle with the defendant, which means we won't have to go to trial. So…"

"*Sooo…*"

"So yes, I'll be staying for the fest."

"*Yeah*!" Scott yelled, wrapping Mina up in his arms and spinning her around.

She squealed loudly and gripped the back of his neck while her feet dangled in the air. As the twirl came to a slow stop, Mina looked down at Scott and gently held his face in her hands. Just as they went in for a kiss, Lillian appeared in the entryway.

"Hey, Mary sent me back here to check out the new merch—"

Mina and Scott abruptly turned toward her, a look of surprise on both their faces. Mina tapped his shoulder, and he quickly put her down.

"Hey, Lillian," he said. "Yeah, come on in. Take a look at all the great new stuff we ordered."

"Never mind," Lillian mumbled, appearing as though she may burst into tears. "I see you two are busy. I can come back later."

"No, you're fine." Mina insisted. "Let me show you—"

"I said never mind," Lillian said, a little snippier this time. "I'll just have Mary show me later."

Mina actually felt bad for Lillian as she watched her slink back inside the café.

"Didn't I tell you she's got a huge crush on you?" Mina asked Scott.

Scott shook his head adamantly. "Look, Lillian and I have a friendly, respectful, employer-slash-employee relationship. That's it."

"Yeah, for you maybe. Clearly not for her. But anyway, we don't have to stand here and debate about that. There's actually something else I want to discuss with you."

"Oh?" Scott moved in closer to Mina and wrapped his arm around her waist. "Does it have anything to do with us picking up where we left off before that little interruption?"

Mina gently placed her hands on his chest. "Um, no. Not quite."

Scott straightened up and dropped his arm. "Okay, what's up?"

"When are you going to tell everyone that The Icicle Café might be closing?"

Scott sighed and took a step back. "I don't know."

"I felt so guilty after talking to Mary about what merchandise to carry in the gift shop year-round. She still doesn't even know the real reason why I'm here, which is to say goodbye to the town on behalf of my family. Nobody does. And now that I've bonded with all these people, the last thing I want to do is make them feel as if I've deceived them."

Scott slowly spun the display tower and stared at the icicle keychains. "I know. I don't want that either. I've just been stalling because I'm convinced that Felix is going to say yes to this deal."

"But what if he doesn't? You can't just spring the news on everyone at the last minute. They've been loyal to The Icicle Café for years and deserve to know what's going on as soon as possible. Because if Felix does say no, The Biltmore Corporation is going to swoop in right after the festival and tear this place down immediately."

"You're right. But I'm choosing to step out on faith. I believe in myself and this brand. And I'm confident that once Felix experiences The Icicle Fest and sees the town of Gosberg in action, he's going to be more than willing to partner with me. Now with that being said, I just want to focus on preparing for the festival."

Mina watched as Scott continued to unload boxes. "All right, then. I'll follow your lead." She reached inside a box, pulled out several mini snow globes and placed them on the shelf. "So what types of floats do the townspeople build for the parade?" she asked in an effort to lift the somber mood.

"Now the floats are crazy inventive," Scott said, his dour expression gradually fading as he handed her a set of crystal bells. "They're so good that it's hard to believe the residents actually construct them themselves."

While he began describing the various decorative sleighs and snow blizzard-themed floats, Mina felt herself growing excited. And for the first time since arriving in Gosberg, the thought of returning to Clover was the last thing on her mind.

Chapter Fourteen

"I'M JUST A bit concerned, that's all," Karen said.

"I'm not," Mina responded confidently. "I spoke with the president of Sayer a couple of days ago. He's very confident that my findings will land them a huge settlement."

She and Karen were in the middle of a video chat, and Mina was determined to keep her cool while Karen updated her on the latest shenanigans at the firm.

"Look, all I'm saying is that you need to get back to Clover as soon as possible. I don't trust Mitch and Jeff. Mitch's assistant told me those two were dissecting your Sayer report, and Mitch asked her to schedule a call with the president of the company as soon as possible."

Mina stopped sweeping eyeshadow across her lid midstroke. "Wait, why would they need to talk to him?"

"My point exactly. They don't. Which means they're probably trying to snatch this case from underneath you just like they did the other two."

Mina sighed and dipped her makeup brush into a pot of matte beige shadow. "Listen, I'm not about to let Mitch and

Jeff send me into a tizzy. I have an excellent relationship with Sayer, and my reputation speaks for itself. They know I'm the best woman for this job. They wouldn't dare bump me off this case for Jeff. We're too close to the finish line and a huge payout."

Karen grabbed her phone and thrust it as close to her face as possible. "I bet you felt that exact same way about the Pitch Perfect and Henderson cases, didn't you? News flash, Mina, this is not a drill. For the first time, I seriously think your partnership might be in jeopardy."

Before Mina could respond, her laptop pinged. An email notification from Scott popped up on the screen.

"*Mina*! Are you listening to me?"

"Of course," she insisted, even though she was focused solely on the computer screen. Mina tapped the message and scanned it as Karen continued to rant in the background.

Hello Icicle Fest Planning Committee! Looking forward to seeing everyone this afternoon. As a reminder, please bring in the Event Participation Forms you've collected from the townspeople who are contributing to this year's festival. We need to begin organizing the vendor booths and deciding the order in which each float will ride through the parade.

As a special treat, Mina and I will be serving up a few new dishes for you all to try that we'd like to serve at the fest. So be sure to bring your appetites, and get ready for some delicious beer-braised bratwurst, currywurst, and sparkling white chocolate lemon truffles. See you all soon!

"...and I just don't know how much longer we can keep this up," Karen said. "Everybody thought you would've been back in Clover by now. Your being gone is making it easier and easier for that slithery little snake to slide right into that partnership. I'm telling you, I think he and Mitch are conspiring against you."

Mina had been so busy reading Scott's email that she'd barely heard a word Karen said.

"Listen, I will only be in Gosberg for one more week. The Sayer case is mine and in no way do I feel threatened by Jeff. We buried him during that video conference when he tried to call me out about the ski machine's leadership boards."

"Now that we did do," Karen interjected.

"And that was all thanks to you. Then Mitch even reaffirmed that I'd done a great job on my report. So once I get back to Clover and negotiate Sayer's settlement, the partners will forget that I was ever even gone. Then before you know it, we'll be at Chateau Rocha with champagne in hand, celebrating my newly appointed partnership."

"I can't wait for that moment."

Mina swiped a couple layers of shimmery nude gloss across her lips and ran her fingers through her hair.

"Okay, I need to get going. I've got a meeting at the café with The Icicle Fest Planning Committee."

"A meeting with the what?"

"The Icicle Fest Planning Committee. The festival is this weekend, and I'm helping Scott prepare for it."

"Oh are you now," Karen purred. She propped her chin

in her hand. "What's the tea, sis?"

"There is no tea. I mean, we're just...you know..."

"No, I don't know. Why don't you tell me?"

"There's nothing to tell, Karen. So don't even start."

"Yeah, okay. I don't believe you. But nevertheless, have fun. And stay open. Don't forget, you're a single lady now."

"Stay open to what? A man who lives almost six thousand miles away?"

"Isn't he moving back to the states once the café is sold?"

"No. He's actually working with an investor to try and keep the café open. But whether it sells or not, Scott wants to stay in Gosberg. He loves it here."

"Really? Well, I guess I can't blame him. From what you've told me, it does sound like a magical little town."

Mina smiled fondly. "It really is. I must admit, I wasn't very pleased when I found out I had to come all the way here in place of my parents considering everything that's going on at work. But since I've been back, I have truly enjoyed myself."

Karen stared at Mina's image sympathetically. "Well, I'm happy to hear that. However, you need to hurry up and get back to Clover. Your career and future are on the line. So have fun at the festival, then come home!"

"I will. And just for good measure, I'll send my favorite partner Stephen a quick email letting him know how well my call went with Sayer's president."

"Good luck with that. He's been out of the office with a

terrible case of the flu, and from what I've heard, he has no idea when he'll be back."

"Oh no," Mina groaned. "So Mitch is running the office by himself?"

"Unfortunately, yes. And Jeff has been following behind him like a little lap dog. It's sickening to watch, really."

A rumble of insecurity churned inside Mina's stomach. "I don't like the sound of that. Those two don't have good intentions, especially when it comes to me making partner."

"I agree. And Jeff is doing all that he can to land that partnership. Are you sure there's no way you can come home sooner?"

Mina tossed her makeup brushes inside the bag and unplugged her flatiron. "I really can't. I've already committed to helping out with the festival. Plus I want to stick around and support Scott if things don't work out with his potential partner and he ends up having to announce that the café is closing."

"Uh-huh. I hear you. And you know what? You're caught up."

"No, I'm not. Why would you say that?"

"Girl, bye. You're so caught up you can't even see straight. You have messed around and fallen in love."

"All right, I've gotta go. Because now you're talking crazy. And I need to get to the café and prepare my lemon truffles before our meeting starts."

Karen sat silently for a moment while rapidly clicking the

button on her pen. "Why am I getting the sneaking suspicion that you're not coming back to Clover?"

"What in the world are you talking about? As soon as everything is done here, I'll be right back there."

"I'll believe it when I see it. But anyway, go ahead. I don't want you to be late for boyfriend's meeting."

"*Anyway*, thank you so much for everything, Karen. From the office intel to all your support, I really appreciate it. And if you hear of any other nonsense going on around the office, I want to be the first to know."

"You most certainly will be. And I'll be sure to keep my eye on those two schemers. Now you go and have a good time with your new man. Bye!"

"Bye, silly!"

Mina disconnected the chat and turned toward her computer. She quickly replied to Scott's email, letting everyone know she was looking forward to the meeting and couldn't wait for them to try her truffles. Then she sent Scott a text letting him know she was on her way to the café.

"Oh, shoot," she said aloud after glancing at the clock and realizing that she should've been at the café twenty minutes ago.

Mina hopped up, grabbed her handbag and computer and rushed out the door. By the time she'd gotten in the car and pulled off, she realized that she had forgotten to email Stephen about the Sayer case.

When she pulled up to a red light, Mina set a reminder

on her cell to send the message. Then she tossed the phone inside her bag and sped off toward the café.

SCOTT STOOD IN the back of The Icicle Café, rifling through the stack of festival participation forms while the planning committee sat at surrounding tables.

"Okay everybody," he said, "I really like this plan that we've put in place. Just to recap, there are a total of eight floats riding through the parade. The sleigh will lead the front of the line, and it'll be followed by the high school marching band. After that will be the two train car floats, which'll be followed by the high school cheerleading team. Next up are the snow blizzard and gingerbread house floats, and they'll be backed by the high school football team. Bringing up the rear will be the snowflake, candy cane, and snowmen floats."

"I think that's perfect," Greta said, who had been co-chairing the festival's planning committee since its inception. "And I spoke with Mr. Beckerman this morning. He's finally agreed to showcase his antique car collection in the parade this year."

"That is epic!" Scott said. "We've been begging Mr. Beckerman to show off that car collection of his since the festival's inception. Mina, could you please add that to the list of confirmed participants?"

"Will do. Are we going to have the cars ride through the parade behind the snowmen float?"

"Yes, that'll work. The cars will bring up the rear. Mary, do we have the final order of the vendor setup?"

"We sure do. The merchants will once again set up over in Union Street Park, and we've got a total of twenty."

"*Twenty*? Wow. That's more than we've ever had."

"I know. This festival just keeps getting bigger and bigger every year! I'll be sure to spread the vendors out so that they won't be competing with one another. We've got holidays crafts, jewelry makers, several specialty food vendors, a few antique dealers, candle makers, and more. The community really outdid themselves."

"They really did," Scott agreed. "I can't thank them or you all enough. This is turning out to be pretty phenomenal, and..."

Mina heard Scott's voice break, and when she looked up, he was rubbing his eyes. She quickly jumped up from her chair and stood by his side.

"I couldn't agree more, Scott," she said, wrapping her arm around him while addressing the committee. "I'm so excited to be able to attend The Icicle Fest for the first time, which actually came as a pleasant surprise since I hadn't planned on being in Gosberg this long. As a matter of fact, I'm probably getting fired from my law firm as I speak!"

When the committee members broke out into laughter, Scott leaned into her ear. "Thank you," he whispered.

"No problem," she murmured before raising her hands in the air and once again addressing the committee members. "So now that we've officially solidified the final details of the festival, who's ready to eat?"

"I am!" the entire group replied.

"Good! Scott and I will go grab the bratwursts that he prepared, along with my white chocolate lemon truffles. We'll be right back."

Mary jumped up and followed the pair. "And I'll grab pitchers of iced tea and water for everyone. Lillian will be over in a sec to take everyone's individual drink orders."

"Thanks, Mary," Scott said.

Mina followed him inside the kitchen. "Hey, are you okay?"

"Yeah. I think so. Thanks for saving me out there. I didn't expect to get emotional like that."

"Of course. And who can blame you? This isn't easy. You're planning a huge annual event with a wonderful group of people who love The Icicle Café. You love it as well, which is making it that much harder for you to face the fact that it may be closing."

Scott took a step toward her. "I know I keep saying this, but, I'm so glad you're here. And not that I'm happy about your father hurting his back or anything, but—"

"Scott!" Mina said, swatting his arm, "You'd better not be happy that my poor father fell off a ladder."

"I'm not!" he insisted through a bellowing laugh. "You

know I'd never play Mr. Richards like that. But seriously, I really do believe that it was meant for you to come to Gosberg. You'd mentioned how your mom said this trip is exactly what you needed. I'm starting to realize that it's exactly what I needed, too."

Mina stared up at Scott. "You know, I have a feeling that even though the café may be sold, this is going to be the start of great things for you."

"I like the sound of that."

Scott placed his hands on Mina's hips and pulled her in close. Just as he gently pressed his lips against hers, she heard someone clear her throat behind them.

The pair quickly pulled away from one another and turned around. Lillian was standing in the doorway, staring daggers at them both.

"Oh, hey," Scott breathed. "What's up? Do you need something?"

"Mary sent me back here to ask if you need help serving lunch to the committee members," she muttered.

Scott looked to Mina. "No, I think we've got it. What do you think?"

"Yes, we can handle it. But thanks, Lillian."

"Mm-hmm," she mumbled before hurrying out of the kitchen.

Mina turned to Scott and covered her mouth. "I am so sorry."

"Sorry for what? I'm not sorry at all. Now, like they say

in all the movies, where were we?"

Mina grabbed his arm and pulled him toward the oven. "You'd better stop being so fresh before we get busted again. Come on. We've got brats and truffles to serve to our hard-working planning committee."

Scott grabbed a stack of plates then handed Mina a pair of tongs. "Why do you always ruin all the fun?"

"You have Lillian to thank for that."

"Facts. But that's okay. I'm gonna get my kiss one of these days."

Mina threw Scott an amused side-eye and remained silent as the pair began filling plates with sauerkraut, grilled corn on the cob, bratwursts and rolls. But in the back of her mind, she had a sneaking suspicion that Scott was absolutely right.

Chapter Fifteen

MINA STOOD NEAR the wall of Alexandra's Day Spa, scanning the various nail polish colors. She picked up an iridescent pink and matte white and held them against her hand, trying to decide which she liked best.

"I like the white," her nail technician Clarissa said. "It'll fit the theme of The Icicle Fest perfectly."

"I think so, too. Let's go with it."

"Excellent. Come on back to my station."

Mina followed Clarissa and took a seat at her manicure table.

"So is this your first time attending the festival?" Clarissa asked her.

"It is. And I'm really looking forward to it."

Clarissa took a seat across from Mina, poured warm soapy water from a pitcher into a bowl and placed her hand inside. "My friend Giselle is on the planning committee, and she shared a lot of the details with me. What stood out the most, though, is the delicious lunch that you all served at the meeting. I was so jealous!"

"I met Giselle. She's really sweet. And don't be jealous.

Everything we prepared will be available at the fest."

Clarissa squealed as she opened a fresh pack of manicure tools and placed them on the table. "Oh good! I love every one of Scott's dishes. And don't even get me started on your desserts. The red velvet cupcakes, the brownies...I've gained a ton of weight since you arrived in Gosberg!"

"Yeah, so have I!"

"But it's been well worth it," Clarissa said with a wink.

The receptionist walked over and tapped Clarissa's shoulder. "I'm sorry to interrupt you," she whispered. "But you have a phone call."

"Could you please tell whoever it is that I'm with a client?"

"It's your daughter. Again. And she said it's an emergency."

Clarissa rolled her eyes and grunted loudly. "When *isn't* it an emergency? I'm so sorry, Mina. Can you please excuse me for a moment?"

"Of course. Go ahead."

"Thank you for being so understanding," she said before removing Mina's right hand from the bowl and placing her left hand inside. "I'll be right back."

After Clarissa rushed off, Mina picked up a magazine and began flipping through the pages. When she stopped and stared at a photo of a stunning bridal gown, a familiar voice approached her from behind.

"Hello, Mina."

She turned around and was surprised to see Lillian standing there with her arms crossed and head cocked to the side.

"Oh, hi, Lillian. I didn't see you when I came in."

"Yeah, I was in the back letting my pedicure dry," she snipped, her entire demeanor cold as ice.

By now, Mina was used to Lillian's standoffish behavior and wondered why she'd even bothered to stop and speak.

"Okay, well…I guess I'll see you at the café," Mina said dryly before turning her attention back to the magazine.

"Are you in the market for a wedding dress?" Lillian asked, her tone dripping with sarcasm.

Stay above it, Mina told herself. *Go high*.

"No, actually," she said without looking up. "Just paging through a magazine while I wait for Clarissa to come back."

"Let me ask you a question," Lillian said.

Mina slowly looked up at her with a blank expression on her face. "Yes?"

"Why did you come to Gosberg?"

Mina's eyebrows shot up. That was the last thing she'd expected to hear. "What do you mean?"

"Exactly what I asked. What suddenly brought you to Gosberg?"

"You do know that I was born and raised here, don't you?"

"Well I was just curious as to why you chose to come now considering you haven't been back to town since high school."

A strange feeling began to buzz around inside Mina's head. She couldn't quite figure out where Lillian was going with this conversation, but whatever direction it was taking, she didn't like it.

"Have you ever heard of the saying, *there's no better time than the present*? Yes, it's been a long time since I've visited. But I just wanted to spend some time in my hometown, check up on the café and attend The Icicle Fest."

"Huh, okay," Lillian said, propping her hand underneath her chin. "I bet you're probably wondering why I'm interrogating you like this."

Mina shrugged nonchalantly. "I guess I am a bit curious since this is the longest conversation we've had since I've been here."

"All right, fine. Enough with all the suspense. I was just curious as to whether your sudden visit has anything to do with the sale of The Icicle Café."

Mina almost choked on the gum she'd been chewing. It felt as if a huge boulder had just been dropped on her head. When she opened her mouth to speak, nothing came out.

"*What*?" Lillian snorted. "No feisty rebuttal from the fancy attorney? Interesting. I'm sure you're probably wondering how I know since you and Scott worked so hard to keep it a secret."

Mina looked around to make sure no one was in earshot. "Yes," she whispered. "I am."

"*Weeell*," Lillian began, her tongue rolling over each let-ter, "Remember when I caught you and Scott in the kitchen making out?"

"We weren't exactly making out, but, go on."

"Before you two realized I was there, I heard you mention that the café is being sold."

Mina swallowed the lump of guilt that had formed in her throat. "Lillian, I'm really sorry you had to find out that way. Scott and I were just trying to find the right time to tell everyone. The café means so much to us all, and—"

"What do you care about The Icicle Café?" Lillian interrupted. "Scott's been the only one who's put any effort into the place. If it weren't for him, it probably would've closed a long time ago."

Mina closed her eyes and took a deep breath. "Listen, Lillian. My mother, along with Scott's, built The Icicle Café purely out of their love for this community. Our parents' unwavering passion is what's sustained the café over the years, in addition to Scott's enhancements."

"Yeah, but—" Lillian said as Mina proceeded to talk right over her.

"And as for me, yes, I have been away for quite some time. But I grew up at The Icicle Café. I spent a ton of time there with my mother, Mrs. Dawson and Scott while learning how to bake and be of service. So regardless of my last visit, the café will always hold a special place in my heart."

"If it's so special to you all, then why are you selling it?"

"Well first of all, the sale isn't final. There's a chance it might stay open. But our parents have decided that they are ready to retire. And as the owners, they have that right."

"Okay, fine. But what if the café *does* close? What about us? When were you all going to let the rest of us in on your little secret? Especially the employees. This is our livelihood, Mina. We all deserve to know. And what about the customers? Some of them frequent the café every single day. They depend on that place for more than just the food. We're like family to them."

Mina's eyes fell to the floor. She blinked rapidly, struggling to hold back tears. Hearing firsthand how much the café meant to Lillian and so many others was heartbreaking.

"You're right," she said through trembling lips. "But Scott and I decided to wait until after The Icicle Fest was over to make the announcement, just in case there's a chance we can save it. If there isn't, we know how excited everyone is for the festival and didn't want to ruin it for them."

Mina paused when Clarissa came rushing back to the table.

"I am so sorry, Mina. This time it really was an emergency. My daughter got into an argument with one of her teachers at school, and I had to arrange for her father to go and pick her up. But I'm glad to see Lillian was here to keep you company."

Mina looked up at Lillian and saw the scowl on her face. "No worries, Clarissa. Hey, would you mind giving us a few more minutes? We were just wrapping up our conversation."

"Oh sure! No problem. I'll go check in with my husband and make sure everything is okay at the school."

"Great, thank you," Mina said before turning her attention back to Lillian. "Look, I know that Scott and I probably could've handled all this differently. But I hope you can understand why we decided to hold off on announcing the news. And again, I apologize that you had to find out the way you did."

Lillian tapped her foot defiantly against the floor. "So when are you going to tell everybody?"

"We're still planning on making the announcement after the festival. But in the meantime, could you please refrain from sharing the news with anyone?"

Lillian clicked her tongue and turned toward the front of the salon.

"Please, if nothing else, do it for Scott. He'd be devastated if the news got out, especially considering he's still holding out hope that the sale won't happen."

"Is that a possibility?" Lillian blurted out, her grim expression suddenly lifting with hope.

"It might be. But at this point, I just can't give you a definitive yes."

"That's not good enough," Lillian insisted just as Clarissa walked back over.

"I'm so sorry, Mina, but I have another appointment scheduled right after yours, and she'll be arriving soon.

Would it be okay if I get started on your manicure now?"

"Yes, of course. My apologies, Clarissa."

"It's fine. We've still got plenty of time. I just don't want to run late." She turned to Lillian, who was busy zipping her coat. "It was good seeing you," Clarissa told her. "I've already confirmed your next manicure appointment on my calendar."

"Thanks," she replied quietly. "See you next week."

"Hey, before you go," Mina said to Lillian, "I just want to thank you for the chat. I hope that we're on the same page, and you're planning on keeping that information you heard to yourself until..."

Mina's voice trailed off as she watched Lillian spin around and walk out of the spa.

"Oh my goodness," Clarissa said. "Why would she walk off like that while you were in the middle of your sentence?"

Mina pulled her cell phone out of her handbag and tapped Scott's contact information. "I have no idea," she lied while composing a text message to him.

We need to talk. Can you meet me at Union Street Park?

Sure, Scott responded almost immediately. *What time?*

NOW!

Okay, you've got me worried with the all caps response. Let me wrap up a few things at the café and I'll meet you there shortly.

"Clarissa, I am so sorry, but now I've got an emergency that I need to go take care of. Would it be too much trouble to reschedule my manicure?"

"No, of course not. Is everything okay?"

“I hope so.”

Mina reached inside her handbag, took out a fifty euro note and placed it on the table. “Thank you so much. I’ll call you soon.”

Clarissa quickly snatched up the money and tried to hand it back to her. “You don’t owe me anything. I didn’t even service you today.”

“It’s for your time and patience. Thank you again!” Mina told her before flying out the door.

MINA SAT ON a park bench overlooking the ice skating rink. When she heard a commotion over by the snack shack, she noticed Scott walking up as a group of teenagers approached him.

“You all ready for the festival this weekend?” he asked them.

“Yep!” they replied in unison. One of the teens approached Scott and placed his hand on his shoulder.

“So Scott, word around town is that Mr. Beckerman’s finally gonna bring out his secret antique car collection during the parade. Is that true?”

“Now where’d you hear a crazy thing like that?” he asked through a sly smile.

“My mom told me. She said she heard a couple of people talking about it around the café.”

"You do know that's top secret information you're trying to get out of me, don't you, Jacob? You'll just have to wait and see."

"Aww, come on, dude!"

Scott laughed and nudged Jacob's shoulder playfully just as the server behind the snack shack counter handed him a cup.

"Hey, Mr. Dawson. Here, have a cup of coffee on me."

"That's so nice of you, Emerson. Thank you. Can I pay you for a second cup for Mina?"

"The Icicle Café's awesome new baker? Absolutely not. Mina's coffee is on the house, too."

"You're the best, Em. Thanks. And I'll be seeing you at The Icicle Fest this weekend, won't I?"

"You sure will. I'll be marching in the parade with the rest of the cheerleading team. We're all really looking forward to it."

"Good. I'm looking forward to it, too. Thanks again for the drinks," he told Emerson before turning to the group of teenagers. "See you guys this weekend."

"See you, Scott!"

Mina stood up as he approached her, giving him a warm hug. "Hey, thanks for meeting me at the last minute."

"No problem. Here's a free cup of coffee from Emerson, who referred to you as 'The Icicle Café's awesome new baker.'"

"Aww, that was sweet of her. Thank you."

"You're welcome," Scott said as he and Mina took a seat on the bench.

"I saw that little exchange you had with the high school kids over by the snack shack. I love how fired up they are for The Icicle Fest."

"I do, too. But it's so bittersweet. Because after this one, that's it. It's all over. And I have to break the news to everyone that the café is closing."

Mina's chest tightened at the thought of having to tell Scott about her exchange with Lillian at the spa.

"Our parents really did something special when they opened The Icicle Café, didn't they?" she asked.

"They sure did…"

He and Mina sat silently for several seconds before he spoke up.

"So what's going on? I'm assuming it must be something important since you asked me to meet up with you at the last minute. *Wait,*" Scott said, grabbing Mina's arm excitedly. "Did you make partner? Is that what this is about?"

"No, No. I wish that's what this was about, but…" Mina folded her hands and squeezed them together tightly. "Actually, I was just at Alexandra's Day Spa and ran into Lillian."

"Uh-oh. I'm guessing she brought up what happened when she walked in on us in the kitchen at the café?"

"She did. But it's not what you think. Lillian actually overheard us discussing the sale of the café."

Scott stared at Mina blankly, as if he hadn't quite grasped what she'd just said.

"What exactly did she hear?" he asked.

"Enough to know that The Icicle Café might be sold."

"Oh no," Scott groaned, dropping his head in his hands. "That's the worst way she could've found out. I feel so bad."

"So do I," Mina said, sliding in a bit closer to him. "But I'm concerned that she won't be able to keep the news to herself and it'll spread before The Icicle Fest. That's why I kept suggesting that you tell everyone beforehand, so to avoid something like this from happening."

"Well did you ask her to keep the news to herself until I make the announcement?"

"I did. But you know Lillian isn't very fond of me. When I asked her if she would please keep the news to herself, she stormed out of the spa without answering me."

"That's not good," Scott said before pulling his cell phone from his pocket.

"No, it isn't." Mina pressed the palm of her hand against her forehead. "I can't stand the thought of being at Lillian's mercy. I wish I would've just broken the news to the town myself when I first arrived in Gosberg."

"Okay Mina, I get it. You think I messed up and should've handled the situation differently. No need to keep dwelling on it."

She leaned back and glared at Scott. "Hold on. Please don't get snippy with me. It's not my fault Lillian overheard us talking. All I'm saying is that this could've been avoided."

Scott typed away on his phone until he looked up at her through steely eyes. "I know it could have, Mina. But thanks to me trying to hold out hope, it wasn't. I can't change that. And now, if things don't go my way, you'll get to go back to your life in Clover while I'll still be here, dealing with the fallout from the café's closing."

Mina parted her lips and blinked rapidly while racking her brain for some sort of comeback. But she couldn't come up with one.

Scott stood up and tossed his cup into a nearby garbage can. "Listen, I need to get going. I'm meeting with Lillian at the café to discuss all this. We've exchanged a few text messages, and she said she hasn't told anyone about the possible sale. I'm pretty sure I can convince her to keep it to herself."

"Okay. Good luck with that."

When Mina stood up and began walking away, Scott reached out and grabbed her hand.

"Hey, wait a sec. I didn't mean to—"

"It's fine," she interrupted.

"Okay…but…I shouldn't have—"

"I said it's fine. You'd better hurry up and get to the café before Lillian changes her mind," Mina insisted.

The minute she climbed inside the car, Mina grabbed her cell phone and began composing a message to Stephen.

Good afternoon. I hope all is well and you're feeling bet-

ter. I wanted to assure you that I will be back in the office first thing Monday morning. In the meantime, are you well enough to schedule a call with me before the end of the week? I would love to speak to you regarding the Sayer case and review the tactics I'm planning to use when negotiating the terms of the settlement with the defendant. Please let me know. Looking forward to hearing from you.

Best regards,
Mina

She read over the message before sending it, then texted Karen.

Hey, I really need to talk. I'm working on scheduling a call with Stephen and planning to be back at work on Monday morning. I could use your help in getting my head back in the game. Let me know if you'll be available in about an hour.

Mina sent the message, then headed back to Emma's. On the way there, she received a text from Scott.

I owe you an apology. I got frustrated and shouldn't have taken it out on you. Please stop by the café tonight for dinner. I'm serving up my specialty, beef short ribs sauerbraten and curried cottage fries. If you can't make it, I hope to see you tomorrow at Walter's Warehouse for the planning committee's float inspection.

Mina shoved the phone inside her purse and sped off, shifting her thoughts back to Stephen and the Sayer case.

Chapter Sixteen

MINA TURNED THE volume down on her cell phone as Stephen coughed loudly in her ear. She tapped the corner of her laptop screen and minimized the Sayer case evaluation report, then pulled up a document that laid out her settlement terms.

Once Stephen finally stopped wheezing, Mina continued.

"Are you okay?"

"I'm fine," he panted. "Please, go on."

"So, one of the main things I want to discuss with Sayer is whether they'd like for me to negotiate a lump-sum payout with the defendant, or arrange a long-term agreement where they'd receive royalties. What are your thoughts on that?"

Stephen emitted a raspy exhale then broke out into a violent coughing spell. "Sorry," he grumbled. "When I last spoke to Sayer's president, he mentioned wanting to go for a lump-sum payout. But it wouldn't hurt to ask which he'd prefer. Are you certain that you'll be back in the office on Monday?"

"Yes," she replied confidently. "I am absolutely sure."

"Well, your reporting on this case has been excellent. You've left no stone unturned. Why don't you go ahead and schedule a call with Sayer for Monday afternoon, and I'll plan on conferencing in from home since I seriously doubt I'll be back in the office by then?"

"I will do that," Mina said, her knees bouncing eagerly underneath the desk. "And I really appreciate you taking the time to speak with me today."

"It's the least I could do. As you know, we hadn't expected for you to be out of the office this long. And It's unfortunate that Jeff took over a couple of your cases in your absence. So I really want to see you get this win, Mina. You know I'm rooting for you."

She held her hand to her chest and took a deep breath. "Thank you so much for saying that, Stephen. I really needed to hear it. I think it's clear to everyone that Mitchell is pushing for Jeff to make partner, so I'm glad to know that I've got you in my corner."

"I would like to think that neither Mitch nor I are playing favorites. At this point, the partnership is still up for grabs. But the excellent work you put into the Pitch Perfect and Henderson cases didn't go unnoticed."

Before she could respond, Stephen hacked loudly into the phone.

"I'd better let you go so that you can get some rest," she told him. "Thank you again for taking my call on such short notice. I really hope you feel better soon."

"Me, too," he choked. "Good luck, and please keep me posted on things."

"I'll be in touch soon."

Mina disconnected the call, opened her email and sent the assistant of Sayer's president a message asking if she could schedule a call with him as soon as possible.

Just when she picked up her cell phone to dial Karen, it buzzed. A text message notification from Scott popped up on the screen.

Hey, I hope all is well, it read. *We missed you at the café last night. The beef short ribs sauerbraten and curried cottage fries were a huge hit. I was wondering whether you're coming to the float inspection tonight. Mary baked crème brûlée sugar cookies, and Lillian is serving up her famous chai latte.*

Speaking of Lillian, I talked to her about the sale of the café. I'll share the details when I see you, which I'm hoping will be tonight. Talk to you soon.

Mina hesitated before replying to the message. She hadn't decided whether or not she should attend the float check. The thought of seeing Scott after their spat at the park made her uneasy, and the fact that Lillian was going to be there only made matters worse.

But Mina had committed to helping out with the planning of The Icicle Fest, and tonight was the last official meeting before the event. The clock was ticking on her stay in Gosberg, and she didn't want to leave town on bad terms. After the festival, she had no idea when she'd return to Gosberg.

Mina closed out of Scott's text and dialed Karen's number, hoping she could help her sort through everything. When she didn't answer, Mina left her a voicemail message then began searching for flights back to California.

Within minutes, her phone buzzed. She assumed it was Karen returning her call. But a text message notification from Mary popped up on the screen.

Hey! it read. *We had so much fun at the café last night, and Scott's special sold out in less than an hour. You were missed! Are you coming to the float inspection tonight? I'm bringing some tasty cookies that I'm dying for you to try.*

Btw, we're almost sold out of ALL the new gift shop merchandise. I placed another order today so that we'll be fully stocked for The Icicle Fest. I'm sure there's more I need to catch you up on. Hope to see you tonight! XOXO

Mina tapped her fingernails against the desk. She turned to her computer and checked her email. There were no new messages. All of her reports and strategies for the call with Sayer's president had been approved. As for Scott and Lillian, Mina knew she couldn't avoid them forever. Plus she wanted to hear about Scott's conversation with her.

Mina replied to Mary's message, then Scott's, letting them both know that she would be at the float inspection.

MINA SLID THE barn door open and entered Walter's Warehouse. She looked around the vast space and gasped while eyeing all the beautifully decorated floats.

Scott was standing over by a huge red sleigh, listening as the owner explained how designing and decorating it had been a family effort.

"Hey, Mina!" someone called out.

She looked toward the back of the warehouse and saw Mary and Lillian standing near a table filled with snacks. Mina inhaled deeply, smiled and waved, then headed over.

Be cool. Be nice, she told herself, curious as to how Lillian would behave toward her.

"Hey ladies," she said, "How are you all doing?"

"We're great!" Mary said before giving Mina a big hug. "How are you?"

"Super busy, but I'm doing well. I had some business that I needed to take care of for the firm this afternoon. But I was able to get everything done, so, here I am."

Mina glanced over at Lillian, who had yet to say a word. "How's it going, Lillian? I heard you're making your famous chai latte tonight."

"I am," Lillian replied with a shy smile that Mina had never seen before. "Would you like to try a cup?"

Mina tried not to appear as shocked as she felt by Lillian's unexpected hospitality. "Sure. I'd love to."

"Okay. One chai latte, coming right up."

When Lillian walked around the table, Mary gave Mina a discreet wink.

"What is going on?" Mina whispered to her right before

Lillian walked back over and handed her a cup.

"Thank you so much." She took a sip of the warm, sweet and spicy drink. "*Wow*. Lillian, this is delicious!"

"Thanks. I'm glad you like it."

"You're welcome. Every drink I've had of yours has been incredible. I hope you know how talented you are. I can actually see you opening your own chain of coffee houses one day. So keep at it."

"Really, Mina?" Lillian said, covering her cheeks with her hands. "That is literally the nicest thing anyone has ever said to me."

Mina was so touched by her reaction that she reached out and embraced Lillian. "Well, it's the truth."

Lillian squeezed her so tightly that Mina felt her breath catch in her chest.

"I'm sorry," Lillian whispered in her ear. "For everything."

"Don't mention it," Mina whispered back. "All is forgiven."

"So does that mean I can get a do-over?"

"Absolutely."

When Mina and Lillian separated, they looked over at Mary, who was dabbing her eyes.

"Will you stop that!" Mina insisted as she began feeling a bit choked up herself. "Hey, where are those crème brûlée sugar cookies I've heard so much about? I need to try them immediately."

"Ooh, yes!" Mary exclaimed. She hurried over to the table, placed a few on a plate and handed it to Mina. "I hope you like them. This is *way* too much pressure. Considering you're now known as The Icicle Café's celebrity baker, it's going to be hard to impress you!"

"Oh please. You've been holding down the café's bakery ever since my mother moved to California, and everyone absolutely adores your baking."

"Now that I can't deny," Mary said before she burst out laughing. "Actually, I think we'd make a great team, wouldn't we?"

Mina paused. She thought about the moments she'd shared with Mary at the café, baking and socializing and interacting with the customers. They brought back warm memories of the time she'd spent working with her mother.

"We'd make a fabulous team," Mina told her, once again struggling to hold back tears. "Now, tell me about these yummy cookies of yours."

Mary smiled brightly and clapped her hands together. "You're going to love them. They're my own personal twist on the original crème brûlée dessert. These cookies are soft and rich, and the creamy custard is surrounded by sweet, caramelized sugar."

"Mm, sounds delish. And I love crème brûlée," Mina said before taking a bite. She closed her eyes and chewed slowly, savoring the moist, buttery goodness.

"Mary! These are *so* good. The cream cheese frosting is to

die for. Please tell me you're going to serve these at The Icicle Fest."

"After the feedback I've gotten today, not only am I going to serve them at the festival, but I'm gonna ask Scott if we can add them to the café menu."

"What's this I hear about adding something to the café menu?" Scott asked as he approached the group.

"Hey!" Mary said. "Mina was just telling me how much she loves my cookies. So I wanted to hear your thoughts on making them a permanent fixture on our dessert menu."

Scott glanced over at Mina. "I uh…I like that idea, actually. I think they'd make a great addition."

"I was so happy to hear that Mary is going to serve them at The Icicle Fest," Mina said. "They're going to blow my poor little white chocolate lemon truffles right out of the water."

"Oh stop it," Mary said, waving her off. "Everybody inhaled those truffles at our meeting within minutes."

"Both desserts are going to be huge hits," Lillian said, glancing from Mary to Mina fondly.

"Aw, thank you," Mina said. She looked over at Scott and noticed that he was staring at her intently. She quickly looked away and focused on her plate of cookies.

Mary took a step back and eyed them both curiously. After a few moments, she abruptly turned to Lillian. "Hey, why don't we go see if the snacks need to be replenished?"

Without giving her a chance to respond, Mary grabbed

Lillian's arm and pulled her away.

"Hey," Scott said, "I'm really glad you were able to make it. Can I take you around and show you the floats?"

"Sure. I'd like that."

The awkwardness Mina expected to feel after seeing Scott was nonexistent. Between his warm, friendly demeanor and Lillian's apology, she actually felt way more comfortable than expected.

"So how are you doing?" he asked, leading her toward the middle of the warehouse.

"I'm doing great. I had a very productive conference call with one of the partners at the firm today. Once I settle my current client's case, I think I'm definitely going to land the partnership."

"That's awesome, Mina. Congratulations."

Just as they reached the floats, Scott took her hand in his and led her to a quiet corner.

"Before we get in the mix and start mingling with everyone," he said, "I wanted to apologize to you in person for the way things went down at the park. I let all this pressure I'm under get to me, and I shouldn't have taken my frustration out on you. So for that, I'm sorry."

Mina caressed Scott's arm. "Thank you for that. I completely understand how you feel, and I accept your apology. Along with that, I'd like to apologize to you as well."

"You would? Why?"

"Because I shouldn't have chastised you for handling

things the way that you did. You've been single-handedly running The Icicle Café for years now, and you know what's best for this community. Considering how much the café means to you, I should have been more understanding of your feelings."

Scott reached out and swept several strands of Mina's hair away from her face. "Thank you. I really appreciate that. And I accept your apology as well."

"You're very welcome."

Mina stood on her tiptoes and looked over his shoulder. She noticed several of the committee members gushing over the floats while climbing inside.

"Are we being rude by standing in the corner whispering amongst ourselves?" she asked.

"We're fine. I just need a couple more minutes. First off, I spoke with Lillian, and she's agreed to keep the news of the sale to herself. We also had a heart-to-heart about you, and I explained to her that you're a great woman who was just trying to do right by our parents. So she gets it."

"Good. Did she also admit to having a crush on you?" Mina teased.

"Of course not," Scott said, chuckling softly. "The jury's still out on that whole theory anyway."

"No, it's not. The jury came back with a guilty verdict. Where've you been?"

"Look, all that's neither here nor there. The bottom line is our secret is safe with Lillian."

"Awesome. And I did notice that she had a completely different attitude toward me when I got here today. Good vibes only. So that was really nice."

"Glad to hear it."

"And what about Felix?" Mina asked. "Does he seem excited about attending The Icicle Fest and the prospect of going into business with you?"

"He does seem pretty amped about attending the festival. But as for going into business with me? I still can't get a good read on that, which is why we're really gonna have to wow him at the festival."

"That's not going to be a problem. Between these fabulous floats and all the other spectacular festivities we have planned, I just can't see him saying no."

"I hope you're right. Because when I even think about standing in front of this community and telling them that The Icicle Café is closing, I get sick to my stomach."

"Then don't think about it," Mina said, caressing Scott's shoulder reassuringly. "Let's stay positive and hope for the best."

He stared at her for several seconds before shaking his head. "*Man* I'm gonna miss you when you head back to California."

"I'm gonna miss you, too."

"Well before we start getting all sappy, let's enjoy this moment and save the sadness for later."

"Deal," Mina agreed.

"Shall we?" Scott asked, offering her his arm.

"Yes. We shall." Mina looped her arm through his and followed him toward the floats.

Chapter Seventeen

"Gosberg High's cheerleading team is phenomenal," Mina said as she and Scott exited the gymnasium.

The pair had just watched a run-through of the team's Icicle Fest routine, and they'd both been completely blown away.

"Yes, they are," Scott agreed. "That squad is nothing like it was back when we were in school. They hired a new coach a few years ago, and she's really focused on the team's athleticism. Now they're on a completely different level."

"All those tricks and flips and splits..." Mina said. "I don't know how they do it."

"My favorite part was that insane pyramid they formed at the end. I held my breath the entire time I was watching."

"Me, too! I didn't think they were gonna pull it off. But they did, and it was flawless."

Mina looked up at the sky. The sun was setting, and the clouds were tinted with beautiful hues of orange and lavender. As a light snowfall filled the air, Scott wrapped his arm around her.

"You know what I suddenly have a taste for?" he asked. "Candied roasted almonds."

"Mm, that sounds good."

"They're great, actually. And it's such a nice night. Why don't we walk over to Hanna's Candies and pick some up?"

"Let's do it."

As the pair headed toward Gosberg's main street, Scott dropped his arm from around Mina's shoulder and intertwined his fingers with hers.

"So, the countdown is officially on, isn't it?" he asked. "All the festivities are coming up, and when they're over, it's back to Clover for you."

"Yes. And time seems to be moving faster than normal. It's funny how I'd only expected to be in town for a few days. And now, even though my trip's been extended, I'm not ready to leave."

"Then don't."

Mina gave his hand a slight squeeze and stared down at the footprints in the snow, unable to say to him what he already knew.

"I know," he continued. "You can't. But I figured it was worth a try. Anyway, I spoke to my parents earlier today. They're still in Belgium, but they'll be back in town in time for The Icicle Fest."

"Good. It'll be nice to see them before I go back to California."

Mina felt Scott's grip on her hand loosen a bit. "And exactly when will that be again?"

"Sunday."

"Hm...okay. I knew it would be soon, but now that it's official, it just..."

"You know what?" she said after his voice trailed off, "Let's not even worry about that. Why don't we focus on the festival and all the fun we're going to have?"

"I think I can do that," he said just as they reached Hanna's.

Scott opened the door for Mina, and when she stepped inside the quaint, nautical-themed shop, the sweet scent of warm chocolate filled her nostrils.

"It smells divine."

"Tastes even better."

The pair walked along the glass counter, eyeing the various fruit jellies, la dolce vita truffles, lemon drops and chocolate coffee beans.

"Do you see anything you want, other than the almonds?" Scott asked.

"Of course I want everything I see. But I'd better just stick with the almonds. At the rate I'm going, none of my suits are going to fit anymore."

"I seriously doubt that. You look perfect."

"Aw, well aren't you just as sweet as all these treats in this case. Thank you."

"Just stating facts. Why don't you go grab a table and I'll place our order?"

"Sounds good."

Mina chose a booth in the front of the shop. Within minutes, Scott came over carrying a tray filled with two bags of candied roasted almonds and two snowman-shaped mugs.

"Ooh, what do you have there?"

"Along with our almonds, I ordered two glasses of glühwein that Hanna just whipped up. It's a spicy apple and tea punch that's mixed with lemons and oranges, and it is absolutely delicious. Here," he said, placing the tray on the table and handing her a mug. "Try it."

Mina took a sip of the drink. "Oh wow. This is *really* good."

"I know, right? I was planning on adding it to The Icicle Café menu. But then, well, you know…"

Mina pointed at Scott. "Remember what we promised. No talking about sad stuff. We're focusing on all things pleasant."

Scott held his hands up. "My bad. On to happier topics. So what's the latest with the law firm? Are things still on track for you to make partner?"

"Things are definitely still on track. I had a call with one of the partners to discuss my current case. Even though he's extremely ill, we were able to review my final reports. He approved of everything, so once I win a settlement for my client, that partnership should be mine."

"I can't wait to get that call from you, telling me that the announcement has been made. That's going to be an exciting moment. Too bad I won't be there to experience it with you in person."

"You'll be there with me in spirit, and I'll be sure to video chat with you that night so that we can have a virtual celebration. How does that sound?"

Scott picked up his mug and held it in the air. "That sounds wonderful. Cheers to your partnership, in advance."

"Cheers," Mina said, clicking her cup against his. "And now, on to these almonds." She reached inside the bag and popped one inside her mouth. "*Scott,* why have you been keeping these a secret from me?"

"Aren't they incredible?"

"Yes, they are. Great choice."

Scott shifted in his chair and shook the bag of almonds. "So uh…I've been seriously thinking about what I'm going to do if things don't work out with Felix and The Icicle Café closes."

"Oh really? What did you decide?"

"Of course I'd love to open my own restaurant at some point in the future. And I'd mentioned maybe doing a pop-up restaurant or starting a catering service. But in the meantime, I'm considering teaching at Gosberg's culinary school. The director is a regular customer at the café, and he's always said I'm welcome to teach there whenever I'd like."

"Scott, I think that's a wonderful idea. You'd be an amazing teacher. Seeing the way you manage the café and conduct the workshops is proof of that. You're so patient and thorough, and everyone really takes to you. I say go for it."

He turned a suspicious eye to Mina. "Hey, are you trying to butter me up so you can steal some of my almonds?"

"Please. I'm not that greedy!" Mina said as she threw an almond across the table.

Scott laughed and quickly ducked. "I'm kidding! I'm kidding. But in all seriousness, thank you for that. It's nice to know my hard work and efforts don't go unnoticed."

"Not at all. The entire town notices and appreciates it."

During the rest of their time at Hanna's, Mina and Scott managed to keep the conversation upbeat and steered clear of any talk about the café possibly being sold. They walked back to the high school parking lot hand in hand and shared a lingering embrace once they reached Mina's car.

"I'll see you at the café tomorrow?" Scott asked.

"Yes, you will."

Scott stared out at the football field. "In the event that Felix decides not to go into business with me, I'll need to make that announcement to the townspeople that the café is closing. Maybe you can help me figure out exactly what I should say. You know, just so that I'm prepared. Because according to my parents, the buyer wants to begin the demolition next week."

"Really? That soon?"

"That soon. And they want to start building out the hotel as soon as possible."

"Whoa. Okay. I'll have to let that sink in. But in the meantime, yes, I will absolutely help you compose the announcement."

"You're the best. Thanks."

Scott took a step toward Mina, and without hesitation, bent down and kissed her. She rocked back on her heels and braced herself, relishing the feel of his soft, full lips on hers.

"Hm," she sighed. "That was nice."

"Yes, it was. And I've been wanting to do that ever since I saw you at the airport."

"*At the airport*? No, you didn't. I haven't forgotten about that funky little greeting you gave me when I first got here."

Scott threw his arms out at his sides. "Come on. Don't do me like that. You know I was just mad because you were only here to rep your parents before they sell the café. But can we please not dwell on that? We've had such a great night. I'd like to end it on a high note."

"And we are," Mina murmured. "See you tomorrow?"

"See you tomorrow." He gave her one last kiss and opened the car door, watching as she climbed inside and pulled off.

On the way back to Emma's, Mina smiled softly and pressed her fingertips against her lips, wondering how in the world she was going to tear herself away from Gosberg.

Chapter Eighteen

EARLY FRIDAY MORNING, Mina and Scott headed to Union Street Park to check on The Icicle Fest setup and make sure everything was going as planned.

"So what do you all think?" the vendor booth coordinator asked the pair. "Looks pretty good, doesn't it?"

"It does, Frank," Scott said. "It looks great, actually."

"I agree," Mina chimed in. "I love it."

The threesome stood in the middle of the park, eyeing all the white tables and tents being assembled around them. The contractor was also handling the festival's signage and decorations, so colorful Icicle Fest banners were being erected throughout the park, along with jumbo wooden icicles, snowflakes, gingerbread men, snowmen, and evergreen trees.

Mina spun around and took it all in. "This looks fantastic. So cheery and festive. It's perfect."

"Good," Scott said, "Because that's the exact look I was going for. Just wait until all the vendors have their booths filled and the park is packed with people. It is quite a spectacular scene."

"I'm glad you two like the layout so far," Frank said. "Once the setup is complete and we get the lights strung on the trees, the entire park is going to look like a glowing winter wonderland."

"Ooh, I can't wait," Mina said, rubbing her hands together excitedly.

"Thanks for all your hard work, Frank. You somehow manage to outdo yourself every year."

"Uh-oh. That means I'll have to come up with an even better concept for next year!"

Mina glanced over at Scott and watched his smile fade a bit. He shoved his hands inside his pockets and cleared his throat. "Next year is so far away. Let's just focus on how great this year's festival is going to be."

"I sure will. Speaking of which, I'd better get back to work. Nice meeting you, Mina."

"Nice meeting you too, Frank."

Once he was out of earshot, Scott turned to her. "I'm telling you, as much as I want to enjoy this festival, I keep being reminded that the café might close, and this could be our last fest."

"Have you ever thought about continuing the tradition of The Icicle Fest even if the café does close?"

Scott shook his head adamantly. "No. It just wouldn't be the same."

"I guess I can understand why you'd—" Mina stopped abruptly when she heard Scott's phone ping.

He grabbed his cell and studied the screen, then covered his face with his hand.

"Oh no," Mina said. "What's wrong?"

"That was a text from my mother. She said that there's a huge blizzard in Belgium, and they don't think they'll make it back to Gosberg until tomorrow. But there's no guarantee that'll even happen."

He turned around and plopped down onto a bench. "I'm really starting to feel the pressure of this situation. I've gotta make a great impression on Felix so that he'll partner with me, my parents may miss the very last Icicle Fest this town might see, you're leaving in a couple of days. And who knows when I'll see you again."

Mina sat down next to Scott and gently placed her hand over his. "But the good news is I'm here now. Trust me, everything is going to work out. In the meantime, let's continue to focus on the positive. The festival setup is coming along beautifully, and the actual fest is going to be fabulous. As for everything else, we'll deal with it as it comes."

"You're right. I need to stay in the moment and appreciate this time, because after this weekend, everything is going to change."

"In a good way," Mina added. "I predict that the next chapter in your life is going to be the best one yet."

"And so is yours, *partner*."

"Hm, I think I like the sound of that."

Scott stood up and offered Mina his hand. "Why don't we do a full lap around the park and check everything out, then head back to the café? I'll whip you up a nice breakfast, then we can finish prepping the bratwursts and truffles."

"Excellent idea," Mina told him, glad to see that his spirits had lifted. "But first, hot chocolate."

"You got it."

And with that she took his hand, and the twosome set out toward the snack shack.

Chapter Nineteen

"THANKS AGAIN FOR going over to the park with me," Scott told Mina after they arrived back at The Icicle Café. "Getting your seal of approval on everything was important to me."

"You're welcome. Glad I could be of service."

Scott took his coat off and hung it on the rack. "I'm gonna run back and check the gift shop inventory. After that, we can have a quick bite then finish prepping the brats and truffles. Sound good?"

"Yes. And in the meantime, I'll be behind the bakery counter harassing Mary and nibbling on a goodie or two."

"Just don't ruin your appetite. I'm making lemon ricotta waffles."

"*Yum*. Can't wait to try them."

Mina strolled around the dessert bar and playfully bumped Mary with her hip. "Don't try and force feed any of your delectables to me," she told her. "You heard the man. I've gotta save room for the waffles!"

Scott threw her an amused look before waving and walking off.

Laughing, Mina turned to Mary, whose forehead was indented with lines of distress. "Hey, you okay?"

"Not really," she replied, both her voice and chin trembling uncontrollably.

Mina leaned in closer. "Mary, what's wrong? Did something happen?"

She sniffled and grabbed Mina's wrist, pulling her into a corner. "*Yes,* something's happened. I heard what's going on," she choked right before tears came streaming down her cheeks.

"What are you talking about? What did you hear?"

As soon as the question was out of her mouth, Mina noticed Lillian bouncing on her toes while peeking over at them. When they made eye contact, Lillian quickly looked away and continued drying a coffee mug.

"What did you hear?" Mina repeated as she felt her limbs go numb.

Mary tightened the grip on her wrist and hissed, "*I heard that The Icicle Café is being sold,*" before emitting a high-pitched sob.

"Oh Mary, I'm so sorry," she said, hugging her tightly. "Scott was planning on telling everyone right after The Icicle Fest. And he would've told you sooner, but he's been trying to find an investor who'll go into business with him and keep the café open."

Mary abruptly pulled away from Mina, her face streaked with black mascara. "Wait, so is there a chance that the sale won't happen?"

"There is. But in all honesty, there's a chance that it will. We're just not sure yet."

"Well, why can't you and Scott just buy the café from your parents and run it yourselves?" Mary whined as her voice began to rise.

Mina patted Mary's back while blinking back tears. "Unfortunately, that's not an option for me. I've got a career to get back to in Clover."

"*Please*. Since you've been in Gosberg you have forgotten all about your career. You've spent way more time working here at the café and living your best life than you have on any of your cases."

"Come on, Mary. That is not true. Or...at least it's not *entirely* true. I mean, yes, I've spent a lot of time at the café. But I've also worked really hard on my caseload, which is why I'm expecting to be named partner as soon as I get back to California."

Mary crossed her arms and glared at Mina. "No offense my dear, but you've been putting way more effort into your baking, the café, and the festival than you have in any of your clients. And don't even get me started on all the time you're spending with Scott. Deny it all you want, but it's clear to me where your real passion lies."

Mina stepped away from Mary and prepared to tell her all the different ways in which she was wrong. But when she tried to formulate the points in her head, they wouldn't quite come together. And when she opened her mouth to speak, nothing came out.

"Hey, Mina!" Scott called out. "I'm done in the gift shop. Meet me in the kitchen when you're done talking to Mary?"

"Okay, I'll be there in a few minutes."

Mina once again noticed Lillian looking her way. This time when they locked eyes, Lillian mouthed the words, *I'm sorry*. Mina ignored her and turned back to Mary.

"So I'm guessing you heard about the sale from Lillian?"

Mary grabbed a bottle of cleanser and sprayed the counter, then rigorously began wiping it down. "I did. But don't be mad at her. I just so happened to overhear her talking about it on the phone with her mother in the ladies room. She was sobbing so loudly that she didn't even hear me walk in."

Mina swallowed hard. She dug her fingernails into the palms of her hands, incensed over the way their two best employees had found out that the café might be closing.

"I'm so sorry, Mary. I really wish Scott and I would've handled things differently. You haven't told anyone else about this, have you?"

She stopped wiping down the counter and peered over at Mina through the corners of her eyes. "I may have mentioned it to a few people," she muttered.

"Oh no," Mina groaned, covering her face with her hand.

"But they swore they wouldn't tell anybody!"

"Mary, nobody is going to keep news this huge to themselves. And if it leaks throughout the town, it'll be a disaster, *especially* the day before The Icicle Fest."

"I guess I didn't think about that…"

"*Miiiina*!" Scott sang out from the kitchen doorway. "Did you forget about me? The waffles are getting cold and we need to get going on the brats and truffles. Can you and Mary finish up your conversation later?"

"Sure, I'll be right there," Mina told him before turning her attention back to Mary. "Listen, I cannot express to you how sorry I am about all this. I'm sure Scott is going to talk to the staff first before he makes any sort of announcement to the rest of the town. But in the meantime, could you please promise me that you won't mention it to anyone else?"

Mary propped her hand on her hip. "Of course. In spite of being completely devastated by the news, I love Scott like a son, and I've grown to love you, too. So from now on, mums the word."

"Thank you, and I love you, too," Mina said before giving her a quick hug then running off to the kitchen.

Mina flew through the door, grabbed Scott's arm and led him into a corner away from the cooks.

"Hey, what are you doing?" he asked, grinning flirtatiously while pulling her in close. "I've got a packed kitchen back here…"

"Listen to me, Scott. Mary overheard Lillian telling her mother that the café is being sold."

"*What*?" he exclaimed, gripping the sides of his head. "You have got to be kidding me!"

"No. I'm not."

"Ugh. I feel awful. I really should've listened to you and handled this differently. Now things are getting out of control. She hasn't told anybody else, has she?"

"According to Mary, she did tell a few people, but they swore they'd keep the news to themselves."

"*Please*," Scott snorted. "I love the people of Gosberg and all, but they don't know how to keep anything to themselves. By the time we get to the festival, the whole town is gonna know about it."

"Well hopefully that won't be the case. So let's just give everybody the benefit of the doubt."

Scott shuffled over to the microwave and placed a tray of waffles inside. "Clearly you've been away for far too long. Have you forgotten how quickly gossip spreads?"

"I haven't," she told him while pulling a couple of plates from the shelf. "I guess I'm just hoping that whoever Mary told will be discreet out of respect for you."

When the microwave beeped, Scott removed the tray and placed several waffles onto each of their plates. He drizzled warm maple syrup over them, then slid a plate toward Mina. "I just hope the news doesn't leak before the festival. If it does, it'll ruin the entire event."

"It won't," Mina said firmly, wishing she felt as confident as she sounded. "Trust me, The Icicle Fest is going to be fantastic. Now let's go eat so we can start knocking everything off of our to-do list."

Scott leaned down and gently kissed her forehead. "See, this is why I'm so glad you're here. I hope you know how much I appreciate you."

"I do," she said, laying her head on his shoulder. "And I appreciate you, too."

After a few moments, the pair pulled away from one another and picked up their plates.

"All right," Scott said, "let's go eat."

Mina followed him out of the kitchen. Just as they sat down, her cell phone buzzed. A text message notification from Karen popped up on the screen.

FYI, Stephen is in the hospital with pneumonia. There have been a ton of closed-door meetings in the office, especially between Mitch and Jeff. I think they're making moves behind Stephen's back. And the president of Sayer came in to meet with them this morning. Something's brewing. I'll keep you posted…

Mina was overcome by a sick sense of helplessness. She felt gutted hearing that Stephen had been hospitalized. And knowing that Mitchell and Jeff had been left to their own devices in his absence was unnerving. Without Stephen, she knew Mitchell and Jeff would continue to steal her clients and take the credit for all her hard work.

Mina hit the reply button and began composing a response.

I could not have been away at a worse time. I'm so sorry to hear that Stephen's in the hospital, and knowing that Mitch and Jeff are sneaking around being shady is really disheartening. I'll send the president of Sayer an email. Hopefully that'll motivate him to keep me on the case. Thanks for the update, and please continue to keep me posted.

"Is everything okay?" Scott asked.

Mina sent the text then plastered a forced smile on her face. "Yeah, everything's fine," she lied, refusing to dump her problems off on him considering everything he was dealing with. "That was just Karen, giving me a quick update on the office."

"And all is well on the work front?"

"Yep. All is well."

"Cool. Let me know what you think of the waffles."

As soon as Mina slid a forkful inside her mouth, Lillian walked over and placed two cups of coffee on the table.

"Right on time," Scott said. "Thanks, Lillian."

She stared down at the table without making eye contact with either of them. "You're welcome," she mumbled before hurrying off.

Mina peered across the table at Scott. "First of all, these waffles are unreal. Secondly, I feel badly for Lillian. I'm sure she thinks I'm blaming her now that the word has spread about the café possibly being sold. I should probably have a talk with her."

Scott slowly wiped his hands with a napkin. "You know, something just dawned on me. I've noticed several customers acting really strange when they came into the café. No eye contact, barely smiling...I bet you more people know than we think."

"I agree. But at this point, what can we do?"

"Make sure that The Icicle Fest goes off without a hitch," Scott told her. "And with that being said, let's finish up so we can get to that checklist."

Mina picked up her cup and took a sip of coffee. After reading Karen's text message, she'd completely lost her appetite. But she forced herself to take a few more bites of food so as not to let on that something was wrong.

In the back of her mind, however, Mina couldn't help but feel as though everything in both Gosberg and Clover was completely falling apart.

Chapter Twenty

MINA STOOD BEHIND The Icicle Cafe's vendor table and looked out at all the townspeople scattered throughout Union Street Park. The festival was officially in full swing. The booths were packed with beautiful jewelry, crafts and artwork. Self-proclaimed chefs and bakers were touting delicious edibles and specialty drinks. The ice skating rink was packed, and various games and contests were well underway.

"Enjoy your brats and truffles, ladies," Mina said to the Stay-At-Home Moms club members. Just when they walked away, Alexandra approached her table.

"Hey, Alex!" Mina boomed. "How are the manicure and massage services going over at your booth?"

Alexandra bowed her head and stared at Mina sternly over the top of her red cat-eye glasses. "The services are going just fine. Thank you for asking," she replied icily.

"Are uh…are you okay?"

"No, not really. May I please have one order of the beer-braised bratwurst, one order of the currywurst, and two orders of the truffles?"

"Sure, coming right up."

Mina waited for Alexandra to give her some sort of indication as to why she was being so cold. When she didn't, Mina realized that she'd probably heard the news about the café being sold.

She placed Alexandra's order on a tray and handed it to her. "Here you go. I hope you enjoy it."

"I'm sure I will. Too bad this is the last meal I'll be able to enjoy from The Icicle Café."

Mina's shoulders slumped in defeat. "I'm so sorry, Alex. Our parents made the decision to sell the café, and Scott wanted everyone to enjoy The Icicle Fest before making any sort of announcement. But there is a chance that—"

"Oh, please, don't even bother," Alexandra interrupted. "The entire town already knows. I'm just surprised you and Scott couldn't put your heads together and figure out a way to keep it open."

"Well that's what I'm trying to tell you. Scott is working to secure an invest—"

"*Hello*, Alexandra!" someone called out. "We're all starving back here. Would you mind moving it along, love?"

Mina stuck her head outside of the tent and saw what looked to be over twenty people standing in line.

"Sorry, everyone!" Alexandra said, waving at the crowd just as Scott walked up.

"Hey everybody!" he boomed. "I hope you're all having a good time."

Mina felt her mood suddenly lift at the sight of him. The energy bouncing off of his bright smile and upbeat demeanor was infectious.

"We're all having a great time," Alexandra gushed. "The food is delicious, and as always, The Icicle Café has the longest line here at the festival."

"Thank you. Glad you're enjoying it."

Scott walked around the table and began helping Mina prepare plates for the crowd.

"Mary will be over in a few minutes to take over so that we can participate in the snowman building contest," he told her. "I was hoping you'd be my partner."

"Of course I will. That'll be fun," Mina said quietly.

"Okay. I know that tone. What's wrong?"

Mina handed Mr. Klein and his wife two containers of truffles. "It's Alexandra," she whispered. "She knows about the sale of the café, and according to her, so does the rest of the town. So now you probably need to address the crowd differently rather than just randomly make the announcement."

"If I can't get Felix to commit to this partnership, then I say we stick to our original plan and make the formal announcement. Everyone still needs to hear the official news from me. But I will include an apology for not letting everyone know what was going on sooner."

"I think that's a good idea. They'd appreciate it. And keep in mind everybody loves you, Scott. They'll understand that your intentions were pure, and you felt as though you were doing the right thing at the time."

"I hope so. Oh, and before I forget, my parents texted me this morning. The snowstorms have passed, so they're definitely going to make it back to Gosberg today."

"Good. I'm so glad they'll be here in time for the festival. Any word from Felix on when he'll be here?"

"He's on the way. I'm expecting to see him any minute now. Are you ready for this? You got your game face on, Richards?"

"I stay ready so I don't have to get ready," she told him just as Mary approached the table carrying a huge stuffed reindeer.

"Hi everybody," Mary said, waving at the crowd before entering the tent. "Everything going okay back here?"

"Yep," Mina chirped, "everything's going great. We're getting awesome feedback on the food and can't seem to keep the line down. By the way, your crème brûlée cookies sold out within the first hour."

"Did they really? I'm so flattered!"

"Now I'll admit, I probably ate half of them," Mina joked, "But nevertheless, they were a huge hit. So how are things going around the park?"

"Fabulous. I won first place in the snowball throwing contest, which is how I snagged this reindeer. Lillian was so jealous. But I told her that her new boyfriend would probably win something even bigger before the end of the festival."

"Wait, *boyfriend*?" Mina said. "Since when does Lillian have a boyfriend?"

"Since she got on some dating app and met a fellow from Frankfurt last week. He's cute, too. His name is Noah. I'm sure you'll meet him at some point."

"I look forward to it. I'm happy for Lillian."

Scott stared across the park then glanced down at his watch. "I think the snowman building contest is about to start. Mary, are you okay taking over for us?"

"Of course. Go on. You two have been working hard enough. Get out there and have some fun."

"Thanks," Mina said, giving her a quick hug. Before she could pull away, Mary leaned in and whispered in her ear.

"Just so you know, the word is officially out. Everybody's buzzing about the sale of the café. And people are really upset. But they're holding it together for the sake of you and Scott, and waiting on him to make the announcement."

"I heard. Don't worry about it. We've got everything covered."

"All right, hon. Go enjoy yourself. We'll chat more later."

Scott took Mina's hand in his, and she followed him toward the other side of the park.

When the pair reached the snowman building station, Scott stopped abruptly and broke out into a huge grin.

"Felix!" he exclaimed, approaching the man and his family. "I'm so glad you all could make it."

"So am I, Scott," Felix replied as the men shook hands enthusiastically. "Thank you for inviting us. Everything looks great. When we visited this park last time we were in town, it did *not* look this amazing."

"I warned you that we pull out all the stops for The Icicle Fest." Scott turned toward Mina and held out his hand. "Felix Becker, I'd like you to meet Mina Richards. She's the daughter of Jake and Lynn Richards, who co-own The Icicle Café along with my parents."

Felix reached out and shook her hand. "Mina, it's so nice to meet you. Scott has told me a lot about you. You're a patent attorney who escaped this snowy town and fled to sunny California, right?"

"That is correct," Mina laughed. "But I must admit, now that I'm back in Gosberg and spending so much time at The Icicle Café, I'm wondering why I ever left."

"I can understand that. This is a lovely town, and not only is the food at the café absolutely delicious, but the theme and setup are fantastic. And speaking of fantastic, please, let me introduce you both to my wife, Gabriele, and our twin daughters, Sophia and Emily."

"It's so nice to meet you," Gabriele said, shaking their hands as the girls waved hello. "Felix and I are really happy to be here and look forward to getting to know the Gosberg community better. And these two rambunctious ten-year-olds can't wait to partake in all these festive activities you've set up."

Felix put his arm around his wife and looked over at Mina and Scott. "And if the feeling is right and we think we can bring something to the town, then who knows what may happen," he said before winking at them.

"Well I know what I'm *hoping* will happen," Scott said before the group burst into laughter. "But seriously, go ahead and check out the festival. I think you'll see that, like your family, the Icicle brand prides itself on high-quality customer service, serving up the best dishes, and continuing time-honored family traditions. For me, it would be a privilege to partner with you."

"That's awfully nice of you to say, Scott," Felix told him. "Thank you."

"You're quite welcome, sir."

"You know, Felix," Mina chimed in, "as I've come to learn more about the Becker brand, I realize that your way of doing business is very similar to the way we've run The Icicle Café through the years. Our parents put a lot of thought and love into the café when they opened it. Then Scott's vision—along with all his hard work, excellent culinary skills, and unwavering passion for the Gosberg community—have taken the Icicle brand to a completely different level. The sky's the limit for how far it could go."

"Wow. I think I like the sound of that. What do you think, Gabriele?"

"I think it sounds fantastic."

"Well go ahead and venture out," Scott said. "Enjoy all

the good food and fun festivities, and we'll reconvene a bit later."

"What do you say, girls?" Felix asked his daughters. "Are we ready to go out and explore The Icicle Fest?"

"Yeah!" Sophia and Emily screamed in unison while jumping up and down.

"Okay then," Felix laughed, "the bosses have spoken. Scott, it's great seeing you again. And Mina, it was really nice meeting you."

"Same here," Scott said as he and Mina shook Felix and Gabriele's hands. "Have fun, and we'll check in with you soon."

The minute Felix and his family were out of earshot, Scott turned to Mina with a megawatt smile spread across his face.

"Could that have gone any better?" he asked before throwing his arms around her. "I mean, seriously, I've got a really good feeling about this."

"I do, too. Felix and Gabriele seem really excited to be here, and I think they're into the idea of partnering with you. But like Felix said, they just have to get a feel for the Gosberg community and figure out whether it would be a good fit for them. How could it not? We *killed* that pitch."

"Yes, we did. But you, my friend, truly knocked it out the park. That bit you added about our vision and passion and taking the Icicle brand to another level? That was genius. *Thank* you."

"You're welcome. But I was just stating facts. Now, are we ready to win their snowman building contest?"

"Indeed we are. Let's do it!"

"OUR GUY LOOKS phenomenal, don't you think?" Scott asked, beaming as Mina tied a red and white checkered scarf around their snowman's neck.

"He really does. I think my favorite accessory is his vintage top hat. Where on earth did you find it?"

"The basement of Rarities Antiques and Collectibles. And while I do love the top hat, I think my favorite accessories are the chocolate chip cookie eyes we decided to go with instead of buttons."

Mina took a step back and inspected their work. "Yeah, that was definitely a unique idea you came up with. Hopefully we'll win extra points for originality."

"Hold on," Mina heard someone say behind her. "It isn't fair that you two are allowed to compete in The Icicle Fest's contests."

Mina spun around and saw Lillian approaching them with a huge grin on her face and a handsome young man on her arm.

"You all are the hosts of the event!" Lillian insisted.

"What fun would it be if we just sat back and watched everyone else have all the fun?" Scott asked.

"And we won't accept any of the prizes if we do win," Mina chimed in. "We just wanted to get in on the action."

"Speak for yourself," Scott told her. "If I win a prize, I'm taking it."

"Will you stop it," Mina laughed.

Lillian wrapped her arm around her boyfriend and brought him closer. "Scott, Mina, I'd like for you to meet Noah. He drove in all the way from Frankfurt just to attend the festival."

"Aw, that was nice of you," Mina said, extending her hand. "It's a pleasure to meet you."

"Likewise," he replied, shaking their hands. "Lillian has been talking about The Icicle Café and this festival ever since we started chatting, so I'm glad I was able to make it."

"Well we're glad to have you," Scott said. "Make sure you stop by the café's booth and grab some bratwursts and white chocolate lemon truffles."

"We definitely will."

Lillian sauntered over to Mina and tugged at her sleeve. "Hey, can I talk to you for a sec?"

"Sure," Mina said before turning to Scott. "Can you hold down our snowman for a few minutes?"

"Of course. Take your time."

Mina eyed Lillian curiously as they headed toward a quiet area near the ice skating rink. She assumed that Lillian wanted to discuss the sale of the café, and what would come of the employees if the deal went through.

But as Mina began debating whether or not she should tell her about Scott's possible partnership, Lillian suddenly threw her arms around her.

"Oh!" Mina uttered before slowly embracing her.

Lillian pulled away and placed her hands firmly on Mina's shoulders. "I owe you an apology."

"*Okay...*"

"I shouldn't have been so rude to you when you first arrived in Gosberg. But I felt threatened. Because I had a huge crush on Scott. *Don't repeat that.* And when I saw the way that man looked at you...I just knew I didn't stand a chance."

Mina's heart thumped so hard that it practically rocked her entire body. "What do you mean?"

"Is that a real question? Wake up, Mina. What I mean is, Scott loves you."

"*Loves* me? I don't know about all that. I mean, I do know that there's something between us. But I haven't fully focused on it because I'm leaving town tomorrow."

"Wait, you're leaving tomorrow? Why?"

"Because I've got a life and a job to get back to in California."

"*Please.* I've barely even heard you talk about California since you've been in Gosberg. You obviously love the life you're living here. This town is in your heart."

Before she could respond, Mina's cell phone buzzed. She pulled it out of her coat pocket and saw a video chat request from Karen appear on the screen.

"I need to take this," she told Lillian. "Can I catch up with you later?"

"Sure. Go ahead."

"Thanks. Oh, and Lillian?"

"Yes?"

"Thank you for that apology. I accept it, and I appreciate it."

"No problem," she replied before waving then hurrying off.

Mina accepted Karen's chat and jogged to the middle of the park.

"Hey girl!" she said, holding her phone in the air and scanning the festival. "You called at the perfect time. The Icicle Fest is in full swing and it's going great. Doesn't everything look fantastic? Can you see the decorations, and all the vendors, and—"

"*Mina*," Karen said, her tone filled with a sense of urgency, "We really need to talk. Can you find a quiet spot?"

Mina dropped her arm and focused on the screen. She noticed that Karen's eyes were red and puffy.

"Of course," she said, rushing toward the back of the park. "What's going on?"

"You haven't checked your email recently, have you?"

"No, I haven't. And I'm afraid to even ask why."

Karen pressed her hand against her chest as her bottom lip quivered. "I hate to have to tell you this, but...Jeff was named partner today."

Mina stopped breathing. Her throat became so dry that she almost choked. "Wait, he *what*?"

"Jeff was named partner. I'm so sorry, Mina."

"But how? How could this happen? Stephen's not in the office, I'm not in the office. There's no way this should've been approved."

"Stephen's absence, along with yours, are the exact reasons why this happened. Of course Mitch spearheaded everything, and according to him, Stephen proxied in his vote through his assistant."

"Can he even do that?" Mina choked, her hand trembling as she covered her mouth in shock.

Karen stared at the screen, her soft eyes appearing sympathetic. "Apparently so. And I can't tell you how terrible I feel. I know how hard you've worked. That partnership should've been yours."

"And let me guess. Jeff is taking over the Sayer case, too."

"That hasn't been formally announced, but considering he and Mitch had a conference call with Sayer's president yesterday that they were fist pumping about afterward, I'm assuming so. Did you ever email the president?"

"I did. And he didn't respond."

A slow, burning anger formed inside Mina's chest. She stood straight up and stomped through the snow. "So what am I supposed to do now? Just stroll back into the office on Monday and act like I'm okay with all of this?"

"Well, you could, because on a positive note, Stephen and Mitch did say that they'd like to name another partner in the next year or so. I'm *sure* it's going to be you next time."

"Next time? I don't think I have it in me to wait that long."

"Keep in mind you've got plenty of allies around the office who respect and care about you. So don't get discouraged. You'll be fine."

Mina felt sick to her stomach. She looked around the park and moaned loudly. "I'm gonna go, Karen. I need to digest all this. I'm just…I'm in shock right now."

"I can imagine. Call me anytime if you need me."

"Thanks. I will."

Mina disconnected the chat, feeling completely lost and confused. She was in no mood to return to the festival. All she wanted was a private moment with Scott to share the news with him.

She saw that he was still standing guard over by their snowman, surrounded by a group of people. Mina sent him a text message asking if he could meet her at The Icicle Café and stressed that it was an emergency.

Without waiting for a response, she practically ran to the café while struggling to suppress a complete emotional breakdown.

Chapter Twenty-One

"MINA!" SCOTT CALLED out, rushing through The Icicle Café's door. "Hey, are you all right?"

She was sitting in a back booth with her head in her hands. "I'm so sorry that I pulled you away from the festival. But I really need to talk to you."

Scott slid inside the booth across from Mina and grabbed her hand. "I'm not concerned about the festival right now. I just want to make sure you're okay."

She snatched a napkin out of the dispenser and dabbed the corners of her eyes. "Thank you. The reason I called you here is because I found out from Karen that I didn't make partner."

"You can't be serious."

"I wish I wasn't. But I am. They named that idiot Jeff partner over me."

Scott jumped up and slid next to her. "Mina, I am so sorry. I know how much that partnership meant to you. And I can't help but think this is partly my fault because I practically begged you to stay in town longer for The Icicle Fest."

"This is absolutely not your fault. I made the choice to stay. I just…I never would've expected the firm to betray me like this. No one even bothered to give me a heads-up before the announcement was made."

Scott wrapped his arm around Mina, and she laid her head on his chest as tears trickled down her cheeks.

"I am literally dreading the thought of having to walk back into that office on Monday. I feel so disrespected, and disregarded, and unappreciated. I have dedicated my entire law career to that firm. So to end up being treated like this is devastating."

Scott leaned down and gently kissed Mina's forehead. "I wish there was something I could say or do to fix this."

"Your being here is more than enough. But seriously, I don't want to keep you from the fest. We can head back."

"Are you sure? Because we can stay here as long as you want," Scott told her just as his cell phone buzzed. He stared at the phone screen and slowly began to smile. "Oh wow. That's Mary texting me. She said they've already run out of bratwursts and truffles and wants to know if we have more. Apparently, the crowd can't get enough and everybody keeps coming back for more."

"Really? But we took a ton of food to the park. I thought we'd end up with leftovers."

"I did, too. We do have that stash in the fridge I was saving for after the parade. But if we take that over now, we won't have anything to serve later."

Mina shrugged her shoulders. "That's okay. Let's give the people what they want. We'll just have to whip up something else tonight."

"All right, then. Let's do it."

Mina stood up and followed Scott into the kitchen. "You know, Mary's message actually made me feel a little better. Knowing how much the townspeople are enjoying our dishes is really heartwarming."

"Now you know how I feel working here every day."

"Too bad I can't say the same about working at the firm."

Scott pulled the brats and truffles out of the refrigerator and set them on the counter. "Well at least you were able to experience it while you were helping out here." He paused and looked over at her. "I still can't believe you're going back to Cali tomorrow."

"Neither can I. But can we please not talk about it? I just want to spend my last day soaking up all of Gosberg's goodness before I have to face the wrath of Clover."

"Say no more," Scott said, grabbing the pot of bratwursts. "We'd better hurry up and get this food back to the festival. The parade will be starting soon."

Mina picked up the container of truffles and followed him out of the kitchen. Just as they reached the front of the café, his parents came rushing through the door.

"Hey my loves!" Betty exclaimed with outstretched arms. "We finally made it!"

"Betty! David!" Mina boomed. "It's so good to see you two!" She set the truffles down and hugged them both.

"It's so good to see you, too!" Betty told her. "How have you been enjoying your time in Gosberg?"

"It's been absolutely amazing. I didn't expect to be here this long, but now that I have, I don't want to leave."

"Well I'm not surprised to hear that," David said. "Gosberg seems to have that effect on everyone. By the way, how is your father doing?"

"Much better. He's almost feeling like his old self again."

"That's good to hear," Betty said. "We were really worried about him. And we appreciate you coming all this way at the last minute to represent your family at The Icicle Fest."

"It's no problem. I'm glad I was able to do it."

"So David and I stopped by the festival on our way here," Betty continued, "which looks marvelous, by the way, and we were bombarded by the entire town!"

"Of course you were," Scott said. "Everybody was probably happy to see you two since you've been traveling so much."

"Nope, that's not why," David replied, crossing his arms in front of him. "Actually, everyone's upset because we're selling this place. I thought you were going to wait until after the festival to make the announcement."

"That was the plan. But unfortunately the news already leaked, and then it just spread all over town."

"Well your father and I weren't the least bit prepared to address the situation," Betty griped. "I mean, everyone is downright irate. And while I do know that this place is special, I had no idea it meant so much to everybody."

"Of course it does," Scott said. "So now that you've been brought up to speed on how much everyone loves The Icicle Café, I've got something I want to share with you two."

"What's up, son?" David asked.

"Well, as you both know, I love the cafe, and I've been against it being sold and torn down since day one."

"*Here we go*," Betty mumbled as she slumped down into a chair. "Just hearing you say that wore me out. You know your father and I are exhausted. So are Mina's parents. Even though you do the majority of the day-to-day work, we're still heavily involved. We're done. Your father and I are ready to move back to the states, travel freely with no obligations, and—"

"I know, I know," Scott interrupted. "Just hear me out. Now, I hadn't mentioned this to you all because I wanted to wait until the possibility became more of a reality."

"What is this boy talking about?" David asked Betty.

"Let him speak, honey," Betty replied before turning back to Scott and waving her hand. "Go ahead with what you were saying."

"Long story short, I have a potential investor who may be willing to partner with me in order to keep The Icicle Café open."

David eyed Scott suspiciously. "So you're saying you've found someone who wants to go into business with you and buy us out?"

"Yes. Possibly. His name is Felix Becker, and he still hasn't made a final decision yet, but—"

"But nothing," his father interrupted. "We've already found a buyer who's ready to close on this deal now. So if this potential partner of yours isn't ready to sign on the dotted line, then he's going to miss out. It's as simple as that."

Scott glanced over at Mina, his eyes filled with worry.

"Mr. Dawson," she interjected, "Felix is actually a well-established businessman. He owns a chain of restaurants in Munich that have been in his family for years. Trust me, he's a serious contender. As a matter of fact, he and his family are at The Icicle Fest right now, getting to know the Gosberg community. Scott and I think that after the festival, he'll definitely be ready to sign on the dotted line."

"Okay, well, just keep in mind that time waits for no one, and neither do I."

"Lighten up, honey, and stop being so negative," Betty said. "Scott, I really do hope that this Felix decides to go into business with you. We may be selling The Icicle Café, but that doesn't mean we don't still love this place. So if we sell it to you, it would be a win-win situation. We'd still collect our profit, move back to the states and enjoy our retirement while you continue the families' legacy by running this beloved community staple."

"Thanks, mom," Scott said before he, Mina and Betty turned to David.

"What are you all looking at me for? Of course I agree with everything you just said, Betts." He chuckled then pointed over at the container of desserts Mina was holding. "What've you got there?"

"These are my sparkling white chocolate lemon truffles. We're serving them at The Icicle Fest. Would you like to try one?"

"I most certainly would." David grabbed a napkin and scooped out a handful. He handed a few to Betty then popped one inside his mouth.

"Mm, mm, mm. Mina, these are delicious! Why haven't we been selling them here at the café?"

"Because we haven't had Mina here to make them," Betty chimed in, closing her eyes and chewing slowly. "But I wish we had, because they're divine. You know Mina, if it weren't for you landing that big partnership at your law firm, I'd suggest you move back to Gosberg and go into business with Scott. The two of you could've pooled your resources together, along with Felix if he wants in on the deal, and acquired The Icicle Café. However, I know how hard you worked to make partner, and that's where your heart is, so..."

A sudden wave of nausea hit Mina out of nowhere. She parted her lips and attempted to tell Betty that she didn't make partner. But she just couldn't bring herself to say it.

"Now that would've been a magnificent idea," David said, reaching inside of the container again and pulling out several more truffles. "Especially after hearing firsthand how badly the town wants to keep the café open and how much you've enjoyed being here, Mina."

Scott gave Mina a sympathetic glance and wrapped his arm around her securely. "Come on, you two. Mina's law career does mean a lot to her, and—"

"No, wait," she interrupted. "Actually, my law career doesn't mean nearly as much to me as it used to."

"What do you mean?" Betty asked. "We thought you loved being an attorney."

"I do. Well I *did* at least. But over the years, my passion for patent law has slowly faded. It's no longer fulfilling. And at this point, I want to be in a warm, respectful environment, surrounded by good, decent people who appreciate my efforts."

"Don't you think that being chosen as the law firm's new partner is a sign of their respect and appreciation?" David asked.

Mina leaned into Scott and stared down at the floor. "I didn't make partner," she finally told them. "The firm decided to go with someone else."

"Oh sweetheart," Betty said, "I'm so sorry. Your parents had given us the impression that it was pretty much a done deal."

"That's what we all thought. But since I've been in Gosberg, one of the attorneys took advantage of my absence and basically pushed me out of the running."

"That's such a shame," David said. "And it's definitely their loss."

"Thank you," Mina told them, mustering up a slight smile. "At least this gives me an opportunity to rethink my plans for the future. Maybe it's time for me to move on from the firm and blaze a new trail."

Mina's cell phone buzzed, and a text message notification from Mary popped up on the screen.

"Uh-oh," she said to Scott. "It's Mary again. We're probably in trouble because we've taken so long getting the food back to the festival."

When Mina opened the message, a photo of all the townspeople standing in front of The Icicle Café's vendor booth appeared.

WHERE ARE YOU AND SCOTT??? the text read. *The entire town has gathered around our table, demanding that you get here with the food ASAP!!! And on a side note, they're all so sad over the possibility of the café closing. It's all they've been talking about…*

Mina was overcome by a heavy sense of guilt. She wrote Mary back, letting her know they'd be there soon. Then she took another look at the photo, studying the joyous expressions on everyone's faces.

And then, out of nowhere, Mina's gloomy disposition suddenly lifted as she was hit with a long-overdue epiphany. She turned to Scott and stared at him through wide, animated eyes.

"What's happening right now?" he asked her. "Why are you looking like that?"

Mina grabbed his arm as her eyes danced wildly. "Because I've just been struck by a huge revelation. You were right. You've been right this entire time. And your parents are right. The entire town of Gosberg is right."

"I'm completely lost. Please clue me in. Right about what?"

Mina strolled toward the middle of the café, opened her arms and slowly spun around.

"Right about the fact that we *have* to keep The Icicle Café open by any means necessary. And you and I should go into business together. Scott, I want to take this place over. With you. And of course Felix too if he wants in. What do you think?"

Scott's mouth fell open. He slowly approached Mina, staring at her while remaining completely silent. After several seconds, he finally spoke up.

"Wait, are you serious? Please tell me this isn't a joke. Are you sure? You really wanna do this? With me?"

"Yes! It's not a joke. And I'm sure. Because ever since I've been back in Gosberg, my entire life has been revived. I wake up every morning excited to start the day. I love being a part of this amazing community. And I've been reminded of just how much The Icicle Café means to me. To everyone, for that matter. Its legacy deserves to live on."

"I mean, I couldn't agree more," Scott said. "But are you *certain* this is what you want? Because it's a huge decision. You're talking about leaving your life and career in California behind and moving back to Gosberg permanently."

"I could not be more certain. This is exactly where I want to be."

Scott wrapped her up in his arms and twirled her around. "Mina Richards, you just made me the happiest man on earth!"

"Oh, this is such magnificent news!" Betty gushed.

"It certainly is," David agreed while continuing to scarf down truffles.

"But wait, what about my parents?" Mina asked the Dawsons. "Do you think they'll agree to this?"

"Of course they will," Betty told her. "I think they'll be ecstatic to hear that the café is staying open and in the family. More importantly, they will be glad to know that you're happy. As parents, that's all we really care about."

"I second that emotion," David chimed in. "So now that you two have a plan, you'd better get back to the festival with the food. Because if you stay here any longer, these truffles are gonna be gone."

"Good idea," Scott said. "Mom, dad, can you two call The Biltmore Corporation and let them know that the deal is off?"

"We'd be happy to," Betty told him.

"I'll call my parents on the way back to the park and tell

them everything that's transpired."

"Good," Scott said. "We need to head out now, because Mary just texted me again saying that if we don't hurry back with the food, she's gonna send the police after us."

"Okay," Mina giggled excitedly. "Let's go."

"We'll see you two at the parade?" Scott asked his parents.

"You sure will," Betty said. "Now hurry up before you're late getting it started."

And with that, Scott and Mina rushed out the door.

Chapter Twenty-Two

MINA AND SCOTT stood outside of The Icicle Café while the parade came to an end out front. The townspeople followed the floats down the street, clapping and cheering as they drove by. Felix and his family approached the pair, each of their faces filled with awe.

"Scott, Mina," Felix said, "You two have truly outdone yourselves with The Icicle Fest. My family and I haven't had this much fun in a long time. Gosberg's energy is magical. And the people are really something special. So, I've talked it over with my wife, and..."

Mina held her breath while Scott raised his eyebrows expectantly. "*And*?" he asked.

"We've decided that we'd love to go into business with you."

"Yes!" Scott said, pumping his fist in the air before sharing an enthusiastic handshake with Felix. "I could not be happier with this partnership. And just to make this deal even sweeter, Mina has decided to move back to Gosberg and invest in The Icicle Café as well."

"*Really*?" Gabriele said. "What huge news! Congratulations, Mina!"

"Thank you," Mina replied, unable to wipe the grin off her face. "I think I'm still in shock, but I am beyond thrilled. I know I've made the right decision."

"I one hundred percent agree with that," Scott told her.

"Well I'm really looking forward to doing business with the both of you and taking the Icicle brand to the next level," Felix said.

"Hear, hear," Scott agreed. "We're going to have to celebrate this moment with a champagne toast later tonight," he told the group just as Mary came running over.

"The parade was so awesome!" she exclaimed. "This has by far been the best Icicle Fest we've ever had."

"I couldn't agree with you more," Scott told her. "Do you think it has anything to do with the fact that Mina helped us out this year?"

"Of course it does. Mina has breathed new life into the café, the festival, and the town overall." Mary looked out at the crowd, the light in her eyes dimming a bit. "But I still can't believe it's all about to come to an end..."

"Just hold tight, Mary," Mina said. "Scott and I have some news to share with everyone."

Mary peered over at her slyly. "What are you all up to?"

"You'll see."

As the crowd gathered around the café, Scott grabbed his bullhorn and turned the volume all the way up.

"*Hellooo*, Gosberg!" he boomed right before the crowd

broke out into more cheers and applause. "Thank you so much for coming out to this year's Icicle Fest. I think we can all agree that this has been the best one yet. That wouldn't have been possible without all of you, the planning committee, our vendors, and the parade participants. You've all been incredible, and we appreciate you!"

Scott paused as the cheering grew louder. He looked over at Mina and grabbed her hand, then raised the bullhorn again.

"I'd like to give an extra special shoutout to Mina Richards. She's been such an integral part of The Icicle Café and has contributed majorly to the planning of the festival. But more importantly, I think we can all agree that Mina's brought an immense amount of joy to Gosberg since the time she arrived. And now, without further ado, I'm going to pass the bullhorn over to her so that she can say a few words."

"Thank you," Mina said before taking over the megaphone.

"Hey, everybody! First off, I just want to thank all of you for being so warm and welcoming since I've arrived in Gosberg. It's really meant a lot to me. My parents wanted to be here as well but my dad injured his back, so they're sending their love all the way from California. As for me, even though this trip was a bit unexpected, it's been life-changing to say the least. I couldn't be happier that I made the trek."

Mina looked out at the crowd and noticed a change in everyone's demeanor. The cheering had stopped and smiles quickly faded. The townspeople looked to one another with uncertainty. She took a deep breath, then continued.

"I'm sure you've all heard by now rumors that The Icicle Café is being sold. Well, Scott and I would like to share with you that they're true. Our parents have decided to sell the café."

Groans and mumbles rippled throughout the crowd. Scott held his hands up and silenced everyone, then gestured for Mina to continue her speech.

"I want you all to know that this café means the world to our parents. But they've owned it for many years, and they're ready to retire. Considering how hard they have worked, Scott and I think they deserve that much. We hope you'll understand and respect their decision to part ways with The Icicle Café."

Louder moans and even a few boos could be heard coming from the group. Mina turned to Scott and Felix and nodded her head, then finally decided to put everyone out of their misery.

"You're probably wondering about the fate of the café," she said.

"We already know!" someone yelled out. "And we don't want some random hotel here in our town!"

As the rest of the crowd joined in on the protest, Scott pressed his finger against his lips. "Come on, everybody! Let her finish."

"Actually," Mina continued, "There won't be some random hotel here in our town. *Because*...Scott and I, along with our new business partner Felix Becker, are taking over The Icicle Café!"

The townspeople fell silent. They looked around as if they couldn't believe what they'd just heard. But when they saw Mina and Scott embracing one another, then shake hands with Felix, everyone broke out into thunderous cheers.

"I am so happy right now," Mina told Scott before handing him the bullhorn.

"Not as happy as I am," he said before once again addressing the crowd.

"In addition to keeping our beloved café open," he continued, "we're planning on expanding the Icicle brand. First up will be our upscale restaurant, The Icicle House."

In the midst of the oohs and aahs, Alexandra stepped forward. "So does this mean that Mina will be moving back to Gosberg permanently?"

Mina gazed up at Scott lovingly. "Yes, it does," she replied. "I'll be moving back to Gosberg as soon as possible."

The crowd erupted in a deafening roar. Scott's mother held her cell phone in the air, and Mina saw that she was streaming a live video chat with her parents. Her father popped open a bottle of champagne while her mother blew kisses at the screen. Mina waved and blew kisses back, then wrapped her arms around Scott.

"So, Ms. Richards," Scott said to her, "what does all this mean for you and me? Are we strictly business partners, or do you see us being something more?"

"I can definitely see us being something more."

"Good. Glad to know we're on the same page," Scott murmured before kissing her softly. But their tender moment didn't last for long once Mary and Lillian bum-rushed the pair, squealing and jumping up and down.

"Ooh, we're so thrilled!" Mary shrieked. "Thank you *so* much for keeping The Icicle Café open. And Mina! I can't believe you're moving back to Gosberg. I knew you were ready to follow your heart and leave that California life behind."

"Yes, you did. I guess I should've listened to you sooner. I could've avoided a lot of turmoil if I had."

"That's okay. Turmoil makes you tougher, and more appreciative of your life once you start living in your purpose," she said, giving Mina's arm an affectionate squeeze before turning to Lillian. "We'd better get inside the café and start preparing for this huge crowd."

"Before you all go," Mina told them, "you have to meet our new co-owner and his family. Felix, Gabriele, I am so pleased to introduce you to two of The Icicle Café's top employees, Mary and Lillian."

"Hello!" Mary beamed, shaking their hands vigorously. "We couldn't be happier to meet you. And take it from me, investing in the café is the best decision you ever could have made."

"We believe you!" Felix laughed. "We're really looking forward to getting to know everyone and working with the Icicle brand."

"We're looking forward to it, too," Lillian said. "Now, if you all will please excuse me, I have to go and call my mom. I'm so ecstatic!"

"Yes, please share the good news with your mom!" Mina told her. "She'll be happy to hear it."

Mary put her arms around Felix and Gabriele. "Would you like to come inside and take a behind-the-scenes tour of the café?"

"Ooh, we'd love to," Gabriele said before rounding up her daughters. "Come on, girls. Let's go check out our new business!"

"We'll see you two inside?" Felix asked Scott and Mina.

"You sure will," Scott told him. "We'll be in momentarily."

After the group walked off, Scott turned to Mina and pulled her in close.

"Can I tell you something?" he asked.

"Of course you can, *partner*. What's up?"

"I love you."

Mina gasped slightly as tears of joy filled her eyes. "Really? Wow. That's actually interesting, because…"

"Because what?"

"I just so happen to love you, too."

Scott gently swept Mina's hair away from her face. "Well that's good to know, Richards. Because I believe you're going to be stuck with me for a very long time."

"I wouldn't have it any other way."

The twosome shared one last kiss before being swallowed up by the townspeople and showered with congratulatory well wishes.

The End

Want more? Make sure to pre-order Denise's next book, *She Gets What She Wants*, out on March 9, 2021!

Pre-order now!

Join Tule Publishing's newsletter for more great reads and weekly deals!

About the Author

Denise N. Wheatley is a lover of happily-ever-afters and the art of storytelling. She has written (and ghostwritten) numerous novels and novellas that run the romance gamut, from contemporary to paranormal, sweet to steamy. Denise strives to pen entertaining stories that embody matters of the heart, while creating characters who are strong, colorful and relatable.

She is an RWA member and received a B.A. in English from the University of Illinois at Chicago, the city where she was born and raised. When Denise is not sitting behind a computer, you can find her in a movie theater, on a tennis court, watching true crime television or chatting on social media.

Thank you for reading

Love at the Icicle Café

If you enjoyed this book, you can find more from all our great authors at TulePublishing.com, or from your favorite online retailer.

CPSIA information can be obtained
at www.ICGtesting.com
Printed in the USA
LVHW010140161220
674261LV00007B/1077